D1047967

The Mann's Back,

playing it low and deadly in a last-chance game of international espionage.

Tiger Mann,

America's superspy, outwits an ace Soviet agent, foils a plot to kill a king, and takes the ruby from the navel of a restless Arabian dancer. All for the good of his country. No one but Mann and his ultrasecret organization could handle such a hazardous mission. No one but Spillane could write such a roaring hell-raiser of a thriller.

"Trench-coated Tiger Mann, easily America's hardest-boiled security agent." —The Saturday Review

"Machine gun pace . . . good writing . . . fascinating tale." —Charlotte Observer

"It is unfair to apply rules to Spillane, who observes only one: that the story must keep you reading." —New York Times

"There's a kind of power about Mickey Spillane that no other writer can imitate." —Miami Herald

SIGNET Thrillers by Mickey Spillane

☐ THE BIG KILL (#P3709—60¢)

☐ BLOODY SUNRISE (#P4018—60¢)

☐ THE BODY LOVERS (#P3221—60¢)

☐ THE BY-PASS CONTROL (#P3077—60¢)

☐ THE DAY OF THE GUNS (#T4178—75¢)

☐ THE DEEP (#T4176—75¢)

☐ THE DELTA FACTOR (#P3377—60¢)

☐ THE GIRL HUNTERS (#D2266—50¢)

☐ I, THE JURY (#P3382—60¢)

☐ KILLER MINE (#P3483—60¢)

☐ KISS ME, DEADLY (#P3270—60¢)

☐ THE LONG WAIT (#T4433—75¢)

☐ ME, HOOD (#P3759—60¢)

☐ MY GUN IS QUICK (#P4112—60¢)

☐ ONE LONELY NIGHT (#P3126—60¢)

☐ THE SNAKE (#T4434—75¢)

☐ THE TWISTED THING (#D2949—50¢)

☐ THE TOUGH GUYS (#T4141—75¢)

☐ VENGEANCE IS MINE (#P3721—60¢)

THE NEW AMERICAN LIBRARY, INC., P.O. Box 2310, Grand Central Station, New York, New York 10017

Please send me the SIGNET BOOKS I have checked above. I am enclosing $_____(check or money order—no currency or C.O.D.'s). Please include the list price plus 15¢ a copy to cover mailing costs. (New York City residents add 6% Sales Tax. Other New York State residents add 3% plus any local sales or use taxes.)

Name_____

Address_____

City_____State_____Zip Code_____

Allow at least 3 weeks for delivery

the death dealers

 *MICKEY SPILLANE*

A SIGNET BOOK from
NEW AMERICAN LIBRARY
TIMES MIRROR

COPYRIGHT, ©, 1965 BY MICKEY SPILLANE

All rights reserved. No part of this book may be reproduced in any form without permission in writing from the publisher, except by a reviewer who wishes to quote brief passages in connection with a review written for inclusion in a magazine, newspaper or broadcast. For information address E. P. Dutton & Co., Inc., 201 Park Avenue South, New York, New York 10003.

Published by arrangement with E. P. Dutton & Co., Inc.

FOURTH PRINTING

SIGNET TRADEMARK REG. U.S. PAT. OFF. AND FOREIGN COUNTRIES
REGISTERED TRADEMARK—MARCA REGISTRADA
HECHO EN CHICAGO, U.S.A.

SIGNET, SIGNET CLASSICS, SIGNETTE, MENTOR AND PLUME BOOKS
are published by The New American Library, Inc.,
1301 Avenue of the Americas, New York, New York 10019

FIRST PRINTING, MARCH, 1966

PRINTED IN THE UNITED STATES OF AMERICA

TO

Jack McKenna and Dorrie

WHO WERE THERE AT THE BEGINNING.

chapter 1

Someplace along the midway of New York they call Broadway I had picked up a tail. I felt it when I crossed Forty-ninth Street and was sure of it by the time I reached Forty-sixth. It wasn't that I had spotted anyone. All you could call it was a feeling, but I *knew*. There had been too many years with too many tails and too many times when I had been behind the other one not to appreciate the crawling sensation that felt like your back was bare to a cold wind.

But why? I had no destination, no assignment. It was just a walk through the city at night. And I wasn't alone. A few hundred people went in either direction between each city block . . . and one of them wanted me.

Without turning around I tried to spot the shadow in the angular store windows and the glass plates over the ads in the theater fronts. Whoever was there had to know I was just drifting so I was able to stop and look over the displays without seeming out of line, at the same time trying to tag the right one.

It wasn't any use. Either I was wrong or there was a pro on the other end. Pedestrian traffic stayed fluid and everyone else pausing at other windows seemed legitimate enough. I eased on down the street, turned right at Forty-fourth until I reached Shubert Alley, then cut over into the areaway between the buildings at a slow walk until I knew I was out of sight, then sprinted past the couples in front of me, ducked into one of the outside phone booths and hugged the phone with the door open so the light would be off, and waited.

I spotted the tail then.

She came into the alley at a normal pace, apparently headed

toward the theater, seemed to frown when she didn't see me, and involuntarily quickened her steps to get to the other end before I was out of sight. When I reached out of the phone booth and flipped her in beside me her face seemed to crack with fright and she almost got a scream started. Then she felt the gun in her ribs and closed her mouth.

We looked real cozy in there—just two people making a joint conversation, one beat-up retread who was a hotshot when the war was on and one beautiful little blonde who looked like she had just stepped out of a chorus line and the gun in her handbag was only to keep the wolves from the stage door. I grinned at her, my mouth tight and dry across my teeth, snapped open the top of her bag and took the flat little Beretta out and dropped it in my pocket.

"Okay, honey," I said, "let's have it."

She only had a second to make it good because I could read any lie she told me and there were too damn many people looking for a piece of my hide to give me any compunctions about crippling somebody if I had to, even if it was a pretty little doll like this one.

There was a strange lilting to her voice when she said, "You are Tiger . . . Tiger Mann?"

"You know that already, kitten. Now who are you?"

"Lily Tornay."

I squeezed her arm and saw her eyes go wet with the pain. "Do better."

"Must we . . . talk here?"

"It's as good as anyplace. I don't like being a target."

"Please . . ." The word came out with a sob.

"Okay, where?" I said.

She looked up at me with big, dark eyes strangely unafraid now. "Wherever you wish."

"How well do you know me?"

"I have been told about you," she said.

"Then you know what will happen if you get cute."

"Yes."

"Don't break away. Walk nice and slow and stay beside me. Get funny and what I do to you will make it look like you fainted and when I have you alone you'll talk up a storm."

She nodded, saying nothing. I edged her out of the booth, shoved my .45 back in the holster and let her feel my fingers bite into her arm above her elbow. Not too far away my friends from the circus were packed into a hotel by the Garden. The show was on now and we could use Phil's room for a couple of hours or whatever it took to see what the little lady had bottled up inside her.

Phil met me on the street under the marquee, handed me his

key with a grin and a few words of wisdom in rapid Mexican and went back to work. Lily Tornay and I took the elevator upstairs to the sixth floor, walked inside and I locked the door behind me.

Then I took the gun out and stood there watching her with it cocked in my hand. I had seen man traps before.

Very deliberately, with the tips of her fingers, she opened her bag, pulled out a wallet and laid it open in her palm.

"Throw it to me," I said.

She tossed it, then sat down with her hands folded in her lap. I snapped it open and looked at the two cards under their plastic covers. One had been issued by our State Department. The other by Interpol. And the names and identification matched.

"You can check my handwriting or thumbprints if you care to," she told me.

I tossed the wallet back on the bed beside her. "Those things can be forged."

"I'm glad you're careful."

"That's why I'm still alive."

Lily Tornay looked at the phone on the nightstand meaningfully. "You know where to call. An agent can be here to identify me in ten minutes."

"I don't need any help, sugar. Where did you pick me up?"

"Outside your hotel."

"Why didn't you make contact there?"

"I wanted to be sure we wouldn't be seen. I followed you. I was going to make the contact in a different manner." She paused a moment, looking at me carefully. "How did you know I was there?"

"I could feel you."

She nodded then. "Yes. I know what you mean."

"Okay, Lily, you've made the contact. What are you after?"

"You. I was told to find you."

"By whom?"

"Teddy Tedesco."

I brought the gun up and leveled it at her head. "You're lying, kid. Teddy's dead. He caught it over a month ago."

"That's what he wanted everyone to think. The dead man carried his ID and the body was too mangled to make an identification positive. They accepted what they saw and he was free to continue with his work."

I let my words out very slowly. "What work?"

Lily shook her head, a frown darkening her eyes. "He didn't say. He told me you would know what to do."

"Knock it off, baby."

"Tiger . . ." She stood up defiantly, staring me down. "I'm

an authorized agent for Interpol cleared by your own State Department. We know of you and your association with Martin Grady and his . . . business associates. These men may be big enough and wealthy enough to operate an efficient civilian spy system that can buy or create political coups or life or death or whatever they want in the guise of patriotism, but too often they have interfered with the machinery of proper governments. There are things happening in this world that are bigger than any wealthy idealists or whatever they are and the outcome is not going to be according to their direction. They have men like you working for them, wild, intelligent, ruthless men who carry out their orders who are sometimes capable of wrecking the whole system with one reckless act."

"Maybe it needs wrecking."

"Not . . . by you people."

"Lily . . . you're getting away from your point," I said. "Teddy Tedesco."

I caught her with that. She sucked in her breath impatiently, tightened her mouth, and let her eyes roam over me before she spoke again. "He is in a position to cause an incident that can lead to nuclear war."

"How about that," I said.

Her mouth dropped open in surprise. "You . . . don't care?"

"Baby, I don't give a hoot in hell. Where is he?"

"Selachin. It's a small kingdom in the Saudi Arabian area."

"Who sent you here?"

"Interpol."

"That isn't a political organization."

"Death *is* their business. Your friend was responsible for several."

"Then nail him."

"We can't. He has disappeared."

"Tough," I said.

She wouldn't buy my tone. There was a hard, fanatical set to her face as she fought to control herself. "Unfortunately, we must make the best of the situation. Tedesco is on what you people call an assignment that can cause war."

"That's his business, not mine."

"But it is your business now, Tiger Mann. It was your friend Tedesco who managed things so we had no choice. He took me at gunpoint and told me I was to find you and say one word. We knew enough about his intentions so that when he carried them out to a certain extent we were past the point of no return and our hand was forced. So I found you."

My hand was tight on the gun now. One wrong word and she was going to be dead on the spot. "Say it, Lily."

"Skyline."

I eased the hammer down on the .45, held it at half-cock and snugged it back in the holster.

Skyline. A coded word that had meaning to four people only, a death-word you passed on when you lost control. Whatever Teddy had was too big to handle alone and he wasn't going to make it himself. He was going to die before he could complete his mission and needed a backup hand at once. It was hot enough to break his cover and jeopardize me, hot enough to go to any extreme to pass on the word for an assist, even to exposing our organization.

You know the meaning of death in this business. You can make it happen and when it comes your turn you're ready to accept it. You know the odds and the meaning of an assignment or you're not part of the group at all. You don't call for help outside your own control unit unless the situation is so critical your own death is relatively unimportant in view of what could happen to the free world. To give a *Skyline* signal meant that it had already happened.

Skyline. Teddy Tedesco's assignment had passed into my hands.

"How long have you been looking for me?"

"I arrived B.O.A.C. yesterday. The State Department office here in New York passed me to I.A.T.S. and they gave me several probable locations. This evening I narrowed down the area without finding you until your former O.S.S. commander, Colonel Charles Corbinet, reached me with the names of several hotels."

"You have a big in, honey. Does I.A.T.S. know what this is all about?"

"I don't know. There are some lapses in communications between your agencies, as you well realize."

"Bureaucracy, the evil thereof," I said. "Do *you* know?"

"At this point, no. My orders were simply to reach you with the message. Interpol is checking out the situation now. By tomorrow morning I will be notified."

"Tomorrow may be too late." I stood there watching her, debating how far I should go. All it would take for me was one single, lousy mistake and I was on the dead list.

Remember the old days, Tiger? You were young and fast and strong. Full of piss and vinegar. Now the vinegar is all gone and all that's left is the piss. If there's still enough left maybe you could drown somebody in it. Twenty years plus since the chute drops into Germany. Twenty years plus since it had all been fun and one big game. Now you survived because time had let you and all the professional techniques had developed into an instinct that made you raise a gun faster and pull

11

the trigger without question and gave you a subtle insight into the innermost workings of another mind. Describe yourself and it came out killer. Describe yourself and it came out like she said: ruthless. Nice word. You could face down the other pros and know that you could do it sooner and more accurately than they could and the twenty years plus added up to number one on the Commie "A" list . . . the Vegolt . . . the one they wanted eliminated more than anybody.

So why expose yourself now, Tiger? The game was almost over. You won your damn letter a long time ago. Money? Sure . . . it was big . . . you were part of Martin Grady's team, subsidized by millions that could buy anything under the sun. Almost. Maybe. The other side couldn't buy you, so it had to be almost.

A few city blocks away Rondine was waiting for you to call. The wedding date was set and the woman you loved, but almost killed once, was there waiting for you to call.

Rondine, lovely, lovely Rondine of the auburn hair and beautiful thighs with a flat belly and breasts that made you gasp at first sight and whom no other could touch, she was waiting for you. Rondine of the wet mouth and fierce desires who wanted you and the soft life where you could live and love without the guns and the fat sound of a bullet plowing into soft flesh.

She was waiting now while you prowled the streets of the city wondering how you were going to tell her that there was no stopping point, no ending to the life you had lived because the original Rondine was just like you.

Dead now. A Nazi spy and dead somewhere in Europe. Confirmed.

Rondine, the oldest of the Caine family, whose ancestry dated back to the nobles who forced the hand of King John on the Magna Carta. Rondine, who defected to the Nazis in '41, was never to live as a Caine again, but simply as Rondine. We had met as enemies and loved with the intensity only enemies can have, but we had loved.

Or rather, I had. She finally shot me twice to kill me quick so she could save her own precious hide and for twenty years I had searched her out. I thought I had found her and she was inches away from death when I knew it wasn't Rondine after all, but her youngest sister, Edith Caine. But she was still Rondine to me and I loved this one even more.

And now she'd have to keep on waiting for me.

I said, "Where are you staying?"

"The Taft."

"For how long?"

"I expect to be recalled in a few days. My assignment ends with reporting my contact with you."

"Get back to the hotel and stay put. I'll check with you in a couple of hours."

"I see no reason . . ."

"And I'm not asking. Interpol might be interested in further information. I'm sure they'll appreciate the gesture."

She hesitated, thinking over the possible ramifications, then nodded. "Very well, I'll be at the Taft." She held out her hand. "May I have my gun back."

I pulled out the Beretta, dumped the shells out of the clip, jacked the one out of the chamber and handed them over separately. Without bothering to reload the piece, she dropped everything into her handbag. "I don't think there's any need to be that careful now."

"You're only allowed one mistake in the business, baby. I made mine a long time ago. After a while survival gets to be a matter of habit and routine."

"And killing," she said. "I made a point of looking into your background. Every department seems to have a file on you, though the details seem rather sketchy. There are more suppositions than facts. In one case you apparently were in two places a thousand miles apart at the same time."

"I'm a crafty bastard."

"You are more than that. You are important because you can be destructive. The power behind you exceeds that of many small governments. One day you are going to be stopped and it will be a beneficial thing. Whoever does it will get many medals, some visible, others in the form of a sigh of relief."

I grinned at her, feeling what was behind her words. She didn't have to say it, but when the type gets wound up it shows around the edges and sometimes it's fun to make them scratch a little. "You don't like men, do you?"

A little flash of fire came into her eyes. "I am not queer, if that's what you mean."

"I didn't ask that."

Her lips seemed to tighten then. "Outside of a simple function I often fail to see what purpose men really serve."

"Maybe if I have time I'll show you," I told her.

"You won't touch me!"

"It's polite to wait till you're asked, kiddo. Now let's cut out."

I left Phil's key at the desk, grabbed a cab outside the Forty-ninth Street entrance of the Garden and rode Lily up to the Taft. She never said a word, just sitting there staring out the window. When I dropped her off I had the driver cruise back

13

to my place, checked out of the hotel and moved downtown seven blocks to the Barnes House and signed in under T. Mann, Los Angeles, California.

It was exactly a quarter to ten.

I called the desk, gave the operator Rondine's number, and heard her lift the phone. The simple word "Hello" was said with the velvety tone that only generations of culture and good breeding can achieve.

"Tiger, sugar."

She felt the tightness in my voice instinctively. "You've found trouble again." It was a statement, not a question.

"It found me."

After a moment she sought her voice again. There was no sting in it now, no recrimination, just that same touch of sadness that had been there the last time it happened like this. "We should have gone away, Tiger. In two more days we would have been married. The trouble couldn't have found you then."

"This one would."

"Yes," she said slowly, "I rather imagine it would."

"Can I see you?"

"It's . . . late."

"Not that late."

"Tomorrow, Tiger." I let her hang up, then eased the phone back on the cradle.

So now I was a slob again, a person who didn't belong in the world. I'd have to go up there and explain. I'd have to look into those purple eyes of hers and lie because she wouldn't understand the truth. She'd be waiting. So was Teddy.

Who came first? Why ask when I knew the answer already.

The National flight out of Washington dropped the new man into La Guardia a few minutes after two A.M. Martin Grady had cleared the contact personally and I was able to recognize him by the bag he carried, a slightly built young guy about twenty-five who could have passed for a travel-weary junior executive about to make a suburban pad for the weekend, kiss an anxious wife and kids hello and have a couple of large belts before going into his routine.

But I knew better when I saw the way he walked and knew that under the gray suit he was one of those stringy types that was all trained muscle and ready to prove he could earn his keep in the organization.

I let him get loaded into the cab and give the driver a destination before I hopped in behind him and said, "Hi, kid, you flying?"

The cabbie started to turn it on, then the guy said, "Low

14

down, man. Keep going, friend." He grinned at me. "Lennie Byrnes."

We shook hands briefly after the identification and I knew he had heard too damn much about me because his eyes were shiny with excitement and he tried too hard to put a squeeze into the grip.

"You got the poop?"

He nodded. "Ears only. When we're in the hotel."

"Your first time out?"

"I've been on office detail until now."

"Stay loose," I told him. "You're just a courier. Maybe later you'll see the big stuff."

"Okay, so I'm anxious. I'm hoping something will happen. After the delivery it's up to you what I do. Until you release me I take orders from you."

"How far has your training gone?"

"The committee had me for six months, after that another six with the lab and three in the field. I was on the Cosmos bit and did the legwork for Hollendale in Formosa."

"Good job. Who was your instructor?"

"Bradley." He grinned at me crookedly. "Seems like you were his. He filled me in on a lot of wild stories."

"He talks too much. Don't let him scare you."

Central had arranged quarters for him at the Calvin, a tenth-floor rear two-room suite, designating him as a representative for one of Martin Grady's various companies. Just the same, we checked the place out completely to make sure it hadn't been bugged. Any of Grady's or his associates' companies were under constant surveillance by Washington teams since the striped pants boys instigated an investigation a few months back, and they could be as instrumental in stopping our action as the Reds could if we let them get that close.

I let him get unpacked, turned the TV up loud enough to squelch our talk, and sat back in the armchair. "Let's have it, Lennie."

He didn't waste words, getting right to the point. "We got the *Skyline* signal through London, but the transmission was slow and we don't know what has elapsed since it was received. Tedesco can be dead by now or not. There's no word on his activity coming through at all. Central thinks that it's a deliberate cover-up. Teddy was there illegally and there's no way of proving he ever entered or came out. Our State Department isn't talking and neither is the bunch over there. We can't squawk and they aren't offering any information. It's as if the entire situation doesn't exist at all."

"That's what I thought," I said.

"Did you know anything about his mission?"

"No."

Lennie nodded. "It was pretty tight, even with us."

"It's always like that, kid."

"Maybe you're familiar with the topography of Selachin."

"Half desert, half mountain range. I've flown over it, that's about all."

"Then you have it right. Anyway, like a lot of those undeveloped areas that are hot spots in the political war these days, they keep gaining importance. About two years ago an enterprising engineer from Indiana uncovered a vast oil reserve in the foothills of the east range of hills. However, it wasn't the usual type of thing. The oil has to be extracted by a new process that one of our major companies has been experimenting with for about ten years.

"Briefly, if this oil field proves out, it puts this previously small principality in a position of equality with Saudi Arabia. That means both the U.S. and the Commie group will be fighting to get control of the field.

"Luckily for us, we had the jump. It was one of our men who found it and our experimental processing is years ahead of anybody else's. To be sure of what we had, Washington sent in two military technicians and began courting Teish El Abin, the King of Selachin, and suddenly this little creep gets off his donkey and blossoms out in Cadillacs. Naturally, the Reds caught the move and scouted around till they found out why. Now it looks like they're romancing Teish, putting the hook into our men until they can gain the time to develop their own process for the oil recovery."

"What happened to the two technicians?"

"Dead," Lennie said. "What else? They were caught in an apparent landslide. Teddy's last report said it wasn't an accident at all. Those boys were murdered."

"Any complaints from State?"

"There couldn't be without revealing their hand. They have to play this one cute. If they accuse the Soviets it will bounce back in a fine propaganda move throughout the Middle East of how we're trying to exploit the poor, poor peasants. Meanwhile, the Reds gain time. They're closer to the operation than we are and have more latitude of action. What Washington is doing is wooing Teish. He's due here in two days for some big festivities and comes in with his hand out like all the rest."

"Any b.g. on the guy?"

"Very little. Until now he's been more like a local chieftain. They have dozens more like him, but he's got an adviser named Sarim Shey who was educated in London and knows all the ropes and this snake is playing for the highest stakes.

16

What Central is afraid of is one thing . . . Sarim Shey is political. When he was a student he tied in with the Commie groups and there's a strong indication he went the Moscow Institute route too. If that's the case, he's strictly leaning toward the Red end."

"What was Teddy's assignment?"

"To see if there was an oil reserve that could be developed and act as a buffer if any of the Soviets moved in. Someplace along the line he was spotted. Central thinks he's dead. They couldn't afford to let him stay alive."

"And now I move in," I said.

Lennie shook his head. "No. You're to stay here. Our intelligence thinks there will be an attempt to knock off Teish El Abin. He has no heirs as yet although he's engaged to some young girl named Vey Locca. If he gets killed control will pass into the hands of Sarim Shey and the stuff will hit the fan. He'll walk off with U.S. loot and practically pass it into the hands of the Soviets. If he makes a deal with our government to experiment with the oil processing, the Reds can simply sit back until it's done, then walk in with a political *coup* and take it away. We think Teish will be more inclined to go along with our side. He's seen some of the Commie infiltration and knows if they get in, his power goes out. He doesn't like that angle a bit. Trouble is, the Commies can't hit him without causing one hell of a disturbance over there because Teish is as much a religious leader as he is political. Whatever happens has to appear to be an overt move on the part of the U.S. so the Soviets can step into the protector role."

"Same old bit."

"And you're elected watchdog."

"What happens to Teddy?"

"Pete Moore has been recalled and is going in on the search." Lennie reached in his pocket for a cigarette and lit it. "In case you're wondering why you're staying on this end . . ."

"That's just what I'm doing," I interrupted.

"You've heard of Malcolm Turos?"

"Number one Commie agent in the Far East?"

"The same, but he's gained in stature the past year. He heads the *Gaspar Project,* a subdivision of KBD that works only primary targets. He's been assigned to this one personally. You may not know it, but you ran into him once in Brazil when he used the name Arturo Pensa."

"Hell, I shot that bastard."

"Right in the neck. You ruined his beautiful operatic voice."

"Tough."

"He used to sing with one of the Russian companies."

"Now he can do bird calls," I said. "I thought I killed him."

Lennie grinned at me. "He wants you, buddy. Word is out he took this job to get over here. He knew about *Skyline* and figured you'd be in on it."

"I'd enjoy that. This time he'll stay here."

"Martin Grady says for you to play this one tight. You're working against their finest. We're getting heat from all directions and can't afford any mistakes. One move in the wrong direction and Washington will have an excuse for an all-out push against us. Some of the heavy stuff we've had over important heads has been nullified by removal of parties involved. Even our pressure groups are finding too much resistance. The eggheads don't like our interference and are fighting to do it their way even if we lose the cold war."

"I know the picture."

"Then it's up to you now. I'll stand by for instructions, the usual channels are cleared and I have the cash ready if you have to lay it out for anything at all. There's a reception for Teish El Abin at noon the day he arrives at the Stacy Ballroom, then the parade, key to the city crap, then the next day a trip to Washington. You can make your contacts at your own discretion."

I nodded, pulled myself out of the chair and stood up. "Okay, Lennie. I'll file my reports through you. If you have anything new from Central I'm at the Barnes House. I may shift around, but Newark Control will always know where I am."

"Right." He got that gleam back in his eyes and added, "If there's any action . . ."

"I know," I said, "I'll call you."

"Thanks, Tiger." He dropped his grin for a moment and looked at me seriously. "Tell me something, how did you get that name?"

"My old man gave it to me. He thought it was a big joke. I had to fight my way around it since I was three years old."

"Ever lose?"

"Once. A girl four years old kicked the crap out of me."

"Oh?"

"When I was twenty-five I met her again." I grinned at him. "I really got even," I said.

I went out, closed the door and stood there in the corridor a moment. There was nothing to be funny about, nothing at all. Five thousand miles away one of my own could be dying a slow and painful death. Or be already dead. And I had to play the cool end.

chapter 2

The early A.M. editions of the papers had a few squibs in them
about the arrival of the foreign dignitaries. None of the news
services had enough information on Teish El Abin to do more
than give a sketchy account of the colorful background of the
country, Teish's position in his kingdom's affairs and its proximity to the major Arabian governments. Each story mentioned his engagement to the younger Vey Locca and his at-
tachment to his chief adviser, Sarim Shey. Only one of the
Washington columns hinted at the reason for his visit and even
then the supposition was closely guarded in ambiguity.

I put the paper down, showered and got dressed. Down below the hotel the symphony of the city had started with the
dawn, garbage cans and sirens announcing a new day. When I
reached the street a few drunks were arguing on the corner
until a beat cop crossed over and they took off mumbling to
themselves. Taxis on the early shift slowed down hopefully at
each corner, checking for possibles. Two hours later you'd get
a go-by with a growl for trying to flag an occupied, but right
now they were on their best behavior. I walked down a way to
the Carnegie Deli, got a Danish and the best coffee in New
York, then took a dime from my change and got into a pay
phone.

Jack Brant was one of the few rugged individualists left.
After the war he took a fleet of Cats into Israel, moved on into
other areas screaming for development, fought flies, heat, dirt
and natives with his team of bulldozers, helped irrigate half
the deserts in the world and wound up in Saudi Arabia with an
oil company until he got disgusted with the political system,
plowed under a couple of gooks who tried to kill him and got

19

out before they could stick his head on a pole in the middle of the street.

I hadn't seen him for five years and he hadn't changed a bit. When he answered he said, "What the hell do you want! You know what time it is?"

"Sure."

One word was enough. He stopped short, said something under his breath, then: "Damn! Tiger! You old son of a sheik! Where the blazes are you?"

"Across the river from you. I didn't think you'd still be in Brooklyn."

"Man, they don't shoot at you over here. Look, what's going?"

"Need help, buddy."

"Oh boy." He laughed then and added, "I'm afraid to ask. The last time you gave me the pitch we mounted fifty-calibers on a Cat and took off after an army. I'm too old for that stuff any more."

"So I won't ask."

"Nuts to you. Where do we meet?"

"How about the Automat on Sixth and Forty-fifth?"

"Give me about an hour and a half."

"Shake it."

How do you say hello to an old friend who played guns with you against a common enemy? How do you say hello to a guy ready to go without being asked even if he wasn't ready any more? You grin, hold out your hand and take it up like there was no time in between the last time and even if the years have left their mark it doesn't show because you know how the other guy is inside and that's one thing that never changes.

I had the coffees ready, but like all the heavy equipment men, he wasn't satisfied until he loaded a tray army style and had it down in front of him. Jack was one guy I could talk to and knew it stopped there. He had seen our operation in action, been part of it twice and knew how we felt. I gave him the details as fast as I could and watched him soak it up, judging each sentence and trying to correlate it with what he knew.

When I finished he sat back, nodded and said, "Where do I fit in?"

"The last time you came back from Saudi you took some of your men with you who begged to get out of there. You smuggled them in, got them new identities and they're still here. Right?"

Jack nodded, frowning.

"They know the dialect of Selachin?" I asked him.

"Hell yes. They're all from that area. They cut out of there and went west into Saudi when we moved in to pick up some scratch. The peanuts they earned was like a fortune to them and when they learned about the good old U.S. it was like they were hearing about Mecca. That's all they ever had on their minds. They broke their backs just to stay with us and when the chips were down they stayed on our side all the way."

"Good. Think they'd buy into this game?"

"Tiger buddy, if I ask them to jump off the Woolworth Building they'd jump. Now get to the point."

I nodded, straightened it out in my mind and said, "I want to meet a ship tomorrow. Teish El Abin and his entourage will be on it. We'll dress those guys in their native costumes, give them the right things to say, and get a first-class introduction to the big chief. Me, I'm going along with them but stay in the background. I'll be a listener. It's funny, but go to another country only one day's flight from your own, meet a country-man and you'd think you were having a reunion with a life-long friend. Teish will be getting a formal reception and all that routine, but I'd like to be there first with a gimmick before the masks can go on. When can we get with your boys?"

"How about this afternoon?"

"Good deal. I'll arrange for the outfits, get a pitch ready and they can rehearse all night. I just want it cool, friend. No pushing. That has to look good. They'll be up against some experts."

"I wouldn't worry about these boys. They've been around a long while and know the angles. Two of them even finished night school. They'll go along. Where do we get together?"

I gave him Ernie Bentley's address in the loft in downtown Manhattan. Ernie was Martin Grady's expert in special equipment, a graduate engineer and chemist, a hobbyist in explosives and more ingenious than Merlin the Magician. By now Central would have alerted him to the new assignments and he'd be thinking in advance. Twice now, he'd come up with gimmicks that saved my neck and made him purr like a kitten with satisfaction. He'd enjoy playing around with this one.

At eight I walked Jack to the corner, then ambled uptown toward the Taft. There was one funny angle called Lily Tornay that had to be checked out all the way. In the lobby I wrote a note, gave it to the desk clerk and saw what slot he stuffed it in. I waited five minutes, grabbed the elevator and took it up to her floor and tapped on her door.

Then I knew why I had the feeling a pro was back of me the night before. Lily was up and dressed, held the door open, but under the towel over her arm I knew she had the Beretta loaded and cocked even though she thought I was the maid, even though she was smiling, ready for anything, and to show her I was just a little bigger pro than she was, I took it away from her again, eased it closed, flipped out the slugs and shut the door behind me.

I said, "You need some lessons, girl."

She never lost her smile. "I never thought so until now." She stepped back, a silent invitation to come in. "What would you have done?"

"Pulled the trigger," I said.

"And if it were a friend?"

"He should know better than to stand in the way."

"Can I have the gun back?"

I threw it to her, letting the shells clatter on the floor. "Sure."

Very deliberately, she picked them up, loaded the Beretta again and made it disappear into her waistband. "Everything I heard about you was true, wasn't it?"

"You never heard everything, sugar."

"What was left out?"

"The good parts." I walked over to the window, yanked the blinds up and stared down at the street. Out of habit I checked the room out while she watched until I came to the dresser, then I knew I found something. The tape recorder was in the bottom drawer inside a simple stationery box, a lead to the mike going over the back of the drawer with the bug hidden behind a front leg. "Careless," I said.

"Interpol expects all conversations to be recorded if possible when we are on a case."

"Baloney. Try training your mind. One day you'll get killed for showing your hand." I snapped the wire from the bug and put it in her hand. "Maybe Interpol is scratching for help these days."

She dropped the smile then. It went easy and she was the same Lily I had in the phone booth a few hours back: hard, nasty, proud of what she was doing and thinking she was doing it well.

"What are you trying to prove?"

"Nothing with you, girl. I just have to watch myself when I get involved with overly dedicated personnel. Sit down."

"Why?"

"You want me to make you lie down? I can talk to you even better then."

She sat down on the edge of the bed fast, her mouth back in that tight thin line, her eyes watching me closely. "You would, wouldn't you?"

"Damn right, sugar. I learned how to deal with broads a long time ago. Either they have something to protect or something to give away to make their points. There's no middle ground. I can play it both ways from the middle with no trouble." I settled back in the chair and looked at her. "Tell me more about Interpol's bit with Tedesco."

"Why?"

"You're looking for it, kid."

"They said you were no good."

"And they were right. Let's keep it all business. We're on the same team for now, assigned to the same project. There's trouble and it has to be stopped. Maybe you don't like Marty Grady's organization or its method of operation, but your orders are to play along and bring home the bacon. Okay, I'm feeding it to you. I'm his chief operative and a prime target for the Soviets. What hits us hits your bunch and someplace somebody dies, either singularly or en masse. If it has to happen, let's hope it happens singularly. There are too many people who can go up in a big mushroom cloud otherwise. You chose your profession the same way I did mine. We don't like the war makers and we hate the ambitious slobs who don't mind walking over corpses just to be the last man in the world. That's a hell of a way to be a dictator. So consider the odds, honey, and level; otherwise we don't lose singularly, but plurally. It's better than en masse but not as good as not at all singularly. Catch?"

"I . . . think I understand. How can I be sure?"

"You read the files, girl."

"Then what should I say?"

"Where does Interpol fit in?"

We sat there for a full thirty seconds while she took her chances. Mentally, she was reviewing the reports, itemizing every detail she had seen on me and trying to place them in their proper niches. She knew the Martin Grady operation and wanted to see how far she could go without exposing her own operation and where it stood in relation to my own. When she decided she leaned back against the pillow and stared at the ceiling.

"Interpol came in as a matter of course. It was an international police setup because certain nationals had been killed and there was a complaint from their embassies. Briefly, when we followed it through, we learned of your man's presence. Teddy Tedesco was identified, tracked, and located. One of our people knew of his association with the Grady organization and all its ramifications, so until we could positively establish the case we walked easily.

"Eventually the details of the thing came to light. They knew Tedesco and sent me in. It was he who passed your *Skyline* signal and had not our group known what you were doing we would have processed it in the usual manner with a direct arrest or a directive to hold him. Like you, he knew our procedure, covered himself and took the chance that it would go through. Our intentions are to hold Teddy Tedesco for the murder of several people and extradite him under international law."

"Balls," I said.

She lifted her head from the pillow. "Please . . . ?"

"You were running scared. You knew he could throw the whole bit into a panic if he wanted to. Don't give me that international-law crap. Law is where and how you find it. If you think we're going to stand by Saudi Arabian law where they chop your hands off for stealing a loaf of bread you're nuts. They try that on Teddy and some bigwig over there is going to have the supreme pleasure of seeing his genitals proffered to him to eat on the end of a stick. Who the hell do they think we are? Damn it, we got what we wanted because we took it from those who couldn't hold it and we did it the hard way. You think gooks with blunderbusses and archaic ideas don't know this? So now we walk the road easy because nobody in the capital wants to disturb the status quo. They'd better learn there're still some left who can lift a head on the end of a pole as well as the poor uneducated can. Goddamn, I skinned a guy alive once and he screamed his state secrets with no trouble at all. Sure, he died, but he died like he killed other people and we got the answers. I want to see our eggheads trying that, or the Peace Corps, or the politicos.

"Girl, we're strictly civilians working to keep this country out of the hands of the garbage heads who want to give it away to the half-asses. We're people who object to punitive income taxes that destroy the brains of the nation and put control in the hands of those who know nothing. Let's say we're right wing . . . like so far right we go through the wall . . . but anything to knock out the destroyers of our country. Damn, but Jefferson or Adams or Teddy R. should see what goes on now. They'd flip."

Whatever she saw in my eyes turned her face into a mask of fright. She sucked her lower lip in between her teeth and held it there, her hand slowly coming up to cover her mouth.

In a half whisper she said, "You're not fit . . . "

"I've been told that before. What you don't understand is that when you play with the death dealers you use the only weapon they understand—violence. It isn't pretty, but it's effective. You train yourself to lose the squeamishness and sense of fair play our society bred into us because the other side was born without it and has a head start in that direction. They can maim and kill and put the world on edge and it's written off to their lack of understanding and culture because they've been held back and exploited by the supposed land-gobbling capitalist nations. Everybody seems to forget that the leaders of these countries are sharp cookies. Most have been Western-educated and with what they were taught and their own native ingenuity, they put the screws to us, their own kind, and live a life of luxury you don't find outside of fairy tales. Right now world security can hinge on just which way one of those jerkwater kingdoms moves."

"You don't . . . solve world problems . . . with killing," she finally said.

"Then tell them that, baby. Let Interpol find out how two of our technicians died over there. Let them check into that supposed landslide."

It caught her off base and her eyes showed it. "How did you . . . nobody was supposed to know. . . ."

"Martin Grady's money can buy a lot of information."

"Yes. I see that." She seemed to be deciding something, then made up her mind. "The death of those men was one reason Interpol was brought in. Tedesco's activities gave us an excuse to probe."

"Then why use you? Interpol has some hot people on the staff."

"Simply because I *am* a woman. The native leaders show a marked preference for Western types."

"You know how fast a woman can disappear there?"

"I'm aware of it."

"You know they still traffic in slaves of all types?"

"Yes."

"Ever hear what happens to the fringe-area showgirl types who take jobs in some of the Latin American countries and get stranded there? You know this is a deliberate setup that eventually leads them right into a real swinging harem where they either go along with the game or wind up dead? I've seen them, kid."

"I was willing to take my chances. Besides, Interpol was behind me."

"Take a look at their killed-in-line-of-duty list. See how many female bodies were recovered from that area."

"What do you suggest?"

"Play it my way until I get a line on their course of action. You have a logical and authorized reason for investigation and if we need police cooperation it can come through you."

"Something Martin Grady's money can't buy?" Lily said sarcastically.

"Wrong, baby. We usually handle our own police action and are equipped for it, but there are other means and when you have them at your fingertips it can make things a little bit easier, that's all."

"And if I don't agree to this?"

I looked at the bed, then down the length of her body. "Take your choice right now, Lily."

Her hand moved toward the gun in her waistband instinctively and I grinned. "I'll take it away again," I said. "You'll suffer the fate worse than death and love it."

For a full ten seconds she glared at me, then something new came into her eyes and a smile cracked the slash of her mouth. It was full-lipped again and blossomed into a gentle laugh. "Tiger Mann," she said, "I think you're bluffing, but I won't take the chance of calling it. You just might rise to the occasion and I would love it and never be able to get away from you. So on that account, I'll agree to be your little lackey as long as I can file a report to that effect."

"Be my guest," I said and stood up. I turned and looked back from the door. "Later you'll be sorry you didn't call my hand," I said.

Her mouth dropped open in a startled laugh of surprise. "Why, you egotistical, miserable . . ."

"Bastard," I finished for her. "I wish somebody would think of something new to call me." I opened the door, stepped outside and pulled it shut. Lily Tornay had some assets that were going to make her a valuable addition to the project.

A cab let me out in front of the U.N. complex at ten-thirty. It was one of those days when there were more visitors than personnel and everyone seemed to be having a coffee break at the same time, each group like a minor caucus of some kind. Nothing big was on the agenda but you wouldn't think so to watch the activity. Great place, this. Ever since it began with the notion it could bring peace to the world, there has been nothing but wars and hatreds building unendingly.

I had started across the lobby when a hand tapped my shoulder. Behind me Charlie Corbinet said, "Hello, Tiger," in that unmistakable growl of his, and when I turned around he gave me that tough, iron grin and held out his hand.

Charlie had been C.O. of our operation during the war, heading up an espionage group he hand-picked for some of the most critical missions assigned. He was no desk colonel then. He made the jumps like the rest of us, fought his way through the occupied territories, and got his medals the hard way. Later they retired him a general because they thought he was too hard an apple to have in a peacetime army with ideas about the Soviet plans nobody wanted to believe. But they got wise after a while. They had to. Right now his civilian occupation as chief of a major corporation was a damn good cover for his position inside I.A.T.S., the newest and the most secret of our security agencies.

I said, "Hi, Colonel. What are you doing here?"

"Waiting for you. I knew you'd be looking for Rondine. Or should I say Edith Caine?"

"She'll always be Rondine to me." I walked over with him toward the wall, both of us, out of habit, picking a spot where we could watch every face in the place. Our conversation looked no more unusual than any of the dozen others going on in various spots. "What's the scoop?"

"Teddy Tedesco. I suppose you've been alerted to the details by now?"

I nodded. "He's a good buddy, Colonel. You trained him yourself the same way you did me. He's in a jam."

"If he's still alive." He stuck a cigarette between his lips and ducked his head down into a cupped match. "In case you're wondering where all the information came from, I'll tell you this. I contacted Martin Grady personally and passed on the choicest morsels." He blew out a cloud of smoke and watched my reaction. He grinned when there wasn't any and went on. "Ted'll need all the help he can get and if word hits the main office I'm the news source I'll catch hell, so keep the lid on."

"I'm not exactly the talkative type."

"Grady said Pete Moore went in after him. Any word yet?"

"Not that I know of. He won't be going in the usual way. Damn, I wished I were on that end of it."

"Pete's a good man."

"Just the same, I'd sooner do it myself. He's worked that area too often. Too many people know his face. Besides, since that affair in Madrid he's gotten trigger-happy. I hope he knows enough to play it soft."

"He knows. The same Martin Grady knows why you should be on this end." Charlie took a deep drag on the butt and let a gray stream trickle through his nostrils. "This is big, Tiger. C.I.A. and I.A.T.S. have teams on it. They know what to expect and they'll cut down any interference."

"They've tried before."

"Not like on this. They want the Grady operation disbanded. Certain people would give their eyeteeth just to get you."

"Like Hal Randolph?"

"Correct. He's top dog now. You didn't make him look any too good the last time out. He's getting his instructions from a congressional committee and has them to answer to."

"Do you know the whole picture?"

"I can figure things out pretty well," he said. "Teish El Abin is going to have a real umbrella over his head. He's going to be guarded like the President. We can't afford a mistake in this case."

"You've heard of Malcolm Turos, haven't you?"

Charlie looked at me quickly. "Grady has some fine sources."

"He has to. The guy wants me. He'll blow this deal any way he can and try for me in the meantime. If Selachin falls to the Reds, we've had it. Turos has the whole Soviet works behind him. He'll be operating here under cover and we can't afford the first move."

"It'll be touchy," Charlie mused.

"How are your agencies going in?"

"Usual protection routine. Cover at all affairs, on the streets, men front and back and limited exposure for his nibs to possible situations. If possible he'll be kept inside where nobody can get to him. All hotel rooms will be selected, bugged and guarded. It will look like the royal treatment but it's strictly a police operation. Washington knows where they stand on this one and is playing it flat out. Now, let me ask this . . . what are you planning?"

"It goes by ear. We have a man in trouble over there. I don't give a fat damn about Teish or anybody else. He's a punk that has a big hand of cards right now and I'm going to get a better one until we get Teddy out if he's still alive."

"And supposing he's dead?"

I turned and looked at him, knowing my face wasn't very pretty right then. "The law of Selachin isn't a life for a life, Colonel. They put you in a public square and do things like stripping the skin from you in inch-wide strips or cutting a hole in your belly, dragging out a section of intestine and letting the dogs pull the rest out. All the while the people throw rocks at you and spit on you, laughing like hell, never realizing that they might be next in line. I think I can figure out something for old Teish. It won't be the first time."

"So, Tiger, the Reds would win after all."

"Not necessarily, buddy. If it comes to that, nobody but me will know about it. There are ways and ways. I think I know them all."

"That's what I'm afraid of," he said seriously. He stuffed the butt out in a chromed stand, then said abruptly, "Have you seen Rondine yet?"

"No."

"She's in the lounge."

"Thanks."

"I saw her a little while ago."

"So what?"

"This has international complications. The British are as interested as we are, perhaps more so. She knows the picture."

"Who filled her in?"

"You know damn well she's a trained, part-time agent. They know where she stands with you and her bunch went directly to her with the details. She's on assignment too."

"Oh?"

"To keep you from underfoot."

"Now it's you with the sources," I said. "Who's side are you on?"

"Right now, yours. For some stupid reason I have the feeling you people are the answer to this trouble. If you weren't qualified to handle it I'd be damn jumpy, but in this case I think you have the edge." He grinned at me. "Damn patriots. You'd think this was still '76."

I winked at him and left him standing there.

The lounge was at the end of the lobby, a small place off limits for visitors but I didn't pay any attention to the sign. I pushed the door open and walked in and there she was, the most beautiful woman in the world, tall, auburn-haired, shoulders wide and trimming down to a narrow waist that flared out in luscious hips and thighs that swelled against the fabric of her skirt.

She stood there, a Coke in her hand, looking out the window toward the stream of people on the street, lost in her own thoughts. I said, "Hi baby."

Rondine turned, startled, her eyes momentarily pinpointed from having looked into the light. Then the irises went large as she saw me there in the shadows. "Hello, Tiger."

I walked over, took the Coke bottle from her hand, and pulled her close to me. There was a nervous tautness in her body that resisted for a second, then she softened and with a small whimper her eyes closed and her mouth was a hungry little animal searching for mine, hot and wet, the tip of her tongue probing for satisfaction that only I could give her. When she let her head fall back and opened her eyes there was that touch of London in her voice when she said, "Damn you, Tiger."

"Sorry, sugar. Things happen."

"When does our wedding happen?" Her fingers bit into my biceps deliberately. "I know . . . what you're thinking."

"So Charlie Corbinet told me."

"The embassy moved me from my translator's job temporarily."

"I heard that too. So you're supposed to bird-dog me."

"It may be the only way I'll get to see you."

"Nuts. I don't like it, kid. Women aren't cut out for this kind of trouble."

"Just the same, you're stuck with me."

I grabbed her wrists in my hands and pulled her back to me again. "When I want to dump a doll it's no trouble. Keep it in mind. Stay pretty and stay off my back."

"Why do you have to do this, Tiger? Why do you and the others like you have to disrupt everything?"

"Disrupt?" I asked her. "We have a man caught in a trap in a stinking, outlandish country that has never known anything but poverty of its own making and now the head of that place is over here with his hand in our pockets never giving a damn for anything except how much he can gouge out of us. Honey, that one guy is worth more than every gook in a mud hut over there. You think I give a damn about what it means? Look, that one guy dragged my tail out of a hot spot one time and to me he's important, not a bunch of white-shrouded slobs."

"Tiger . . ."

"When it's over I'll be back."

I thought there would be recrimination or tears or a burst of anger at least, but there were none of these things. Then I saw the same expression I had seen on Lily Tornay's face, that of a woman with a job, dedicated, intense. She had been like that when I met her and she was like that again. Her job at the U.N. as a translator was only a cover one. In London she had been trained as an operative and now they were calling on her and I was the assignment.

Rondine reached out and touched her hand to my face, one finger tracing the scar there. "Let me help, Tiger."

"By taking me out of action?"

"Our people are cooperating on this."

"That's not enough. We were there first. We'll be there at the end. I'm an old hand at this, honey. Guns are no games for girls."

"You're leaving now?"

"That's right. I figure on picking up a tail before I get out of the building. No matter how good they are I'll shake them in thirty minutes. Tell them not to waste their time or mine either." I ran my fingers through the silken mass of her hair. "Think you can still kiss me?"

She smiled again, ran the pink tip of her tongue across the ruby of her mouth and lifted her head so I could taste her again. Her entire body seemed to melt against me, her breasts, firm and high, cushioned between us. She took her mouth away, buried her head against my neck a second, then drew back. "All right, Tiger. I love you."

"I love you, kid. Let's hang on to it."

"It won't be easy," she said.

"Nothing good comes easy," I told her.

chapter 3

It only took fifteen minutes to ditch the tail I had waiting. Apparently the cabbie had experience in this thing before and needed little help from me. When he let me out at the subway station I gave him a five spot for his trouble and took a downtown train to where Ernie Bentley's lab was and walked up the street.

From the outside it was just another loft taken over by a small independent business and enough cartons went in and out to make it look legitimate. Once past the squalid foyer you got a different impression. The place was a combination laboratory, darkroom and office with strange gadgets in the process of development standing around like toys in a kid's bedroom. Dr. Frankenstein could have had a ball there.

Jack Brant and his crew hadn't arrived yet, but Ernie had the costumes ready, authentic, colorful and laid out in several sizes. Newark Control had relayed a message to him that Pete Moore had made a successful entry into the area outside of Selachin but no further word had been received on the progress of the mission. On his own, he researched and assembled as much information as he could on the situation there, the highlight of it all being the necessity for a male heir to Teish El Abin's throne. His two previous wives had died at early ages without giving him issue and typically it was blamed on them rather than a probable impotency on the part of their potentate. How Vey Locca was going to work her marital rites would be a cute deal, but it wouldn't be too much trouble for a smart cookie to suddenly show up in a family way regardless of her husband's capabilities. It was an angle to consider.

Ernie's warning buzzer went off then and he went out to let

Jack and the others in. I introduced Jack and let him do the rest. The three with him were short, dark men, smiles reaching all the way across their faces, and from the way they looked at me I knew Jack had filled them in, most likely with a few embellishments, on the times we were together. He ignored their native names which were lengthy and nearly unpronounceable, calling them Tom, Dick and Harry. Rather than resent it, they seemed to enjoy their sudden Americanization. All three spoke good English barely touched with an accent, but could drop back into their native tongue at the drop of a hat.

Jack asked, "What's the program, Tiger?"

"We'll meet the ship," I said. "We'll arrange it so your boys here will be spotted and I'm betting Teish invites us past any police lines to have a chat with the home-town folks."

"Look, these boys have no passports. I told you they were smuggled in."

"And this is New York, buddy. When somebody called it a melting pot they meant just that. There are as many people wrapped in sheets anymore as Ivy League suits. If there's any trouble we'll cut and run. They'll be dressed under the wraps in case we have to make a fast switch. I'm going along for the ride. For the time being I can be a deaf mute. Ernie will dye me their color and a pair of sunglasses will take care of the eye color. I want a firsthand look at all three of them."

"Any reason?"

"Yeah, a big reason. I want to read their dogtags. I want to see what's back of their heads. I want to feel their hands and see how their eyes move. I want them to remember me the next time they see me."

"You're going to stand out, Tiger. You're head and shoulders over my boys."

"I've seen some big ones over there."

"Sure, all eunuchs."

"So I'm a eunuch then. We're playing this by ear, but I want first crack."

"You got it."

"Fine. Then get up a script. I want the boys to welcome Teish with all the pomp they can put on. I want them to do it so nicely there will be a chance the king will go so far as to invite them to a private audience."

"Come off it, Tiger. These guys are peasants to him. Damn dogs in his eyes."

"And this is the U.S. where you don't show preference. He'll have a chance to make himself look good and if he's thinking right he'll fall in line. I've seen it happen before. If we fluff it, we'll try something else, but let's use what we have first. Tell your boys this . . . if it works and the end result is satisfactory, I'll make sure they can legalize their stay here."

Jack grinned at me and relayed the message. Their smile got even bigger and Jack said, "If you want, they'll die for you, too."

"I don't want that. Just talk. Okay, get them fitted out, then go put them through their paces. Teish comes in on the *Queen* at nine-thirty in the morning. We'll meet right here at eight, make sure everything is ready, then go down there together."

"Righto. Things are looking up. You want me to cover your back?"

"Nix. No guns. If we get patted down I want it to be clean. You too."

"Okay, laddie, you're asking for it."

"That's the only way to get anything."

At six o'clock I called Rondine. I let the phone ring a dozen times before I hung up, then tried her office at the U.N. After a couple of minutes I got the tired voice of a cleaner who told me everybody had left an hour ago and wouldn't be in until tomorrow.

For some reason I felt edgy, little fingers of doubt crawling their way up the curve of my spine. Under my coat I could feel my shoulders tighten and it was an old feeling I had learned not to ignore a long time ago. I pulled out the small pad, found Talbot's number and fingered a dime out of my change and dropped it in the slot.

Talbot was a British agent assigned to a minor job at the U.N., always on call as Rondine was, a man of independent means who could support his hobby. He had been wrapped up with me before and had sense enough to know when the chips weren't falling right. I got him on the second ring, heard him say in that Oxford accent, "Talbot here."

"Tiger Mann. Were you on the job today?"

"There I was. What's on your mind?"

"Did you see Rondine leave?"

"I had coffee with her just before she left. Say, you scratched our man beautifully. He lost you within four blocks. But we'll pick you up again. Wish you wouldn't do that. It makes us look bad."

"Tough. Look, where was she headed?"

"Right back to her apartment, old boy. She had an armload of work she planned on getting ready for tomorrow. You know what she's up to, of course."

"Yeah, and I don't like it. She isn't there."

"She must be. I invited her to supper but she refused. She was going straight back." He stopped, then his tone changed.

"What's happened?" he asked softly, his accent almost gone. Suddenly he had become all pro too.

"I don't know. Hop down to the U.N. Check out the cabs and contact anybody who saw her leave. I'll check out her apartment."

All he said was, "Got it," and hung up. I grabbed a cab on the corner, gave the driver her address and perched on the edge of the seat impatiently until we came to her building. I flipped a buck over the seat, hopped out and ran into the building.

It was one of those places with an oversize doorman who didn't like to be budged. He started to put out his hand until he saw my face, then backed off. I said, "Ron . . . Edith Caine . . . did she get here yet?"

"Miss Caine came in quite some time ago, sir."

I didn't wait. I grabbed his arm and spun him around. "Come on."

For a second I thought he was going to object. The cords stood out on his neck and he let me have the kind of grin he used in the ring, his broken nose and thick ears punctuating the smile, then his eyes slitted and he nodded curtly and ran in after me.

The elevator seemed to take forever reaching her floor and I squeezed out the door while it was still half open, ran to her door and punched the buzzer. I knocked, tried the bell again, and nothing happened.

The doorman said, "What's the trouble, buddy?"

I took out the .45, cocked it and put it against the lock without answering him. One blasting shot took all the metal away and left a gaping hole in the woodwork and a rap with my heel smashed it open all the way. I went in with the gun ready in my hand, saw her lying on the floor and flipped the .45 to him and pointed to the bedroom. He picked it out of the air, getting my point without being told and started checking the rooms.

She was alive, but in five more minutes she would have been dead. The thin nylon cord strapping her hands and legs behind her had been looped up around her neck and with every motion she made it drew tighter until it was almost buried beneath the flesh. Her face was flushed and her breath came in weak rasps at jerky intervals as she fought for survival.

I shoved the doorman away before he could touch her. Any extra motion could be the final one, even to trying to unknot the cord. Luckily, she had rolled so that her feet were jammed up against the legs of a heavy chair and even with the spasms of a cramp she had been unable to jerk too much. I eased her feet back to take the pressure off the noose, snatched out a pocket knife and forced the blade under the nylon at the back of her neck and cut it.

She sucked the breath back into her lungs with a deep, involuntary gasp that was almost a sob, nearly choking on the air. I cut loose the rest of the nylon, lifted her to the couch and stretched her out there.

"Wet a towel," I said. "Get a glass of water too."

"Listen, maybe we should call the cops."

"Damn it, do what I told you."

He gulped, his face still pale. "Sure, Mac."

I ran my fingers through her hair and pushed it away from her face. "Rondine . . ."

Slowly, her eyes fluttered open.

"Don't talk. You're okay now."

Her smile was weak, but her eyes told me everything. When the doorman came back I wiped her face until she was breathing normally and the tension was gone, then I let her sip from the glass until she said, "Thank you. I . . . I'm all right now."

"I should call the cops, Mac," the big guy repeated. "This stuff . . ."

When I turned around I let him have the hard stare. My coat opened just enough so he could see the speed rig and the butt of the .45 again and when I said, "What the hell do I look like to you?" he gave me a dumb grin like he had just missed the boat.

"Sorry . . . I'm gettin' slow. I thought you was at first. You ain't from this precinct, are you?"

"I'm from downtown. Now let's get some fast answers. How many people have come in and out of here the past half hour?"

He shrugged, furrowed his eyes in thought and said, "Not countin' the residents, maybe twenty."

"Repeaters?"

"Some. Don't know them by name, but some were here before."

"Could you identify them?"

"Big tippers I can. Few gimme a buck to a fin to open a damn cab door. Them I know."

"Start refreshing your memory then. Think of the ones who didn't tip." I looked down at Rondine. The suffused look was gone now and her face was pale, her lips dry. "Can you talk or is it too much to ask?"

"I can . . . talk, Tiger."

"Okay. Go slow and easy. What happened?"

She pointed to the water glass and I gave her another swallow. She took it gratefully and lay back again, her eyes closed.

"About . . . twenty to six . . . the bell rang."

"From downstairs or here?"

"This door."

The doorman said, "He must've come in behind one of the others. The downstairs door had to be opened with a buzzer then. I was on the curb outside."

"Go ahead, doll."

"I answered. He asked . . . if I were Edith Caine and said he had a message from my office."

"You invited him in?"

Rondine nodded. "He had a briefcase. He opened it . . . but what he took out was a cosh."

"A what?" the doorman asked me.

"British term for a sap, a blackjack."

"Oh."

"He simply hit me," she said. "I was tied up when I regained consciousness."

"What did he want?"

She frowned, her eyes drifting to mine. "Nothing . . . from me. He said, 'You're my gift to Mr. Mann. I owe him more, but he will . . . appreciate this gift.' "

"Describe him."

"Tall . . . thin. He looked . . . rather nice. Nothing special about him that way. Sort of . . . like a businessman. You might say, average except for . . . well, his hair was combed in that manner foreigners seem to have. Just . . . different enough so they don't look . . . American."

"I know what you mean."

"Then there was . . . his voice," she said.

"What about it?"

"Strange. As if he found it hard to talk. Not like having a cold . . . but forced."

I felt the ice run right down my shoulders into my fingertips again. So Malcolm Turos had found my weak link. His information was great, his sources reliable. His little gift of Rondine's death was for my gift of a bullet in his neck. But he had missed. His gift wasn't acceptable and he'd have to try again. He was enjoying his assignment and even when he would learn that she still lived he'd enjoy it because he knew I'd be sweating and my hand couldn't be in the game all the way because I'd have to play cover for her as well as take care of myself and our own project. He would split the action this way and had she died he knew I'd blow my own job to go after him and a guy that comes at you mad is a dead guy before he starts. But he played his openers too cute. He'd let the story go out purposely and a lot of eyes would be on the game because he wanted them to watch him smirk while he cleaned house on me. He was forgetting the old dodge about he who laughs last, lasts best.

I said, "Cool it, baby. No more talking."

She shook her head, watching me closely. "You . . . know who it was?"

"That's right."

"What are you . . . ?"

"I'll take care of it my way." I got up, walked to the phone and dialed the Calvin. I got Lennie Byrnes on the phone, gave him the address and told him to get over as fast as he could.

The big doorman was watching me, taking everything in. I took him to one side and said, "Anybody with a screwy voice say anything to you at all?"

He hunched his shoulders, then shook his head. "Nope."

"See anyone with a briefcase? Tall, thin . . . average guy?"

"Maybe six or eight. A lot come in here like that." He paused, scowled again, then added, "Come to think of it, them what had briefcases been here pretty much before. Like they got clients or somethin' in the building. Only one guy I never seen. Yeah, I remember that one guy now because he looked up at the marquee like he was checking the name of the building and he had a pink scar on his throat about the size of a nickel. He came right in behind the Wheelers. They was getting out of a cab and he came walking."

"You'd recognize him again?"

"Sure would."

"All right, then I'll give you some information and it's to stop right where you are, understand?"

He nodded and grinned. "I get the pitch."

"If he comes in here again you stop him cold. The hard way. Do it out of sight. Get him in the lobby or in the elevator. The guy's armed and dangerous so watch yourself."

"I've had 'em like that before."

"Don't press your luck on this one. This is more than a city police matter. If he gets away from you, or you can't get to him, call the local precinct station and make it an emergency because that's what it will be."

"Got it."

I took out my pen, wrote the phone number of Charlie Corbinet and the I.A.T.S. offices down and put mine on the bottom. "These are Federal Agency people. You get everybody you can on this if it comes up. My number is the last one. You may not be able to reach me, but try anyway. I'm assigned to this job and will be right with it . . . but remember, in an emergency, you go directly to the police and these numbers."

He took the card, checked it and stuck it in his pocket.

"Can I ask you one question, Mac?"

"Go ahead."

"Who're you?"

"My name's Tiger Mann. It won't mean anything to you."

He stared at me through squinting eyes, then started a slow grin. "Like hell it don't." The grin got bigger. "You ain't no real cop either."

"Oh?"

"Remember Maxie McCall?"

"Sure. He still fighting?"

"No more. He's running a gym. Him and me used to be in the army together. Plenty of times he told me about you. Damn, I thought he was makin' it all up."

"He probably did."

The guy gave a sidewise glance toward Rondine on the couch. "Not after this. I believe everything he told me now."

"Keep it to yourself," I said.

"I learned how to shut up a long time ago, Tiger. I better get back downstairs."

It took Lennie fifteen minutes to get there. I had time to reach Charlie Corbinet, give him the layout and tell him to alert I.A.T.S. and the C.I.A. that Malcolm Turos had arrived but to keep his source quiet. He didn't like it, but went along anyway.

Lennie got the picture in a hurry, glad of being involved even if the big action was already over and nodded at my instructions to stay with Rondine every minute she was here. He was to escort her to work and back and stay on tap at the U.N. buildings within reach, even if it was unlikely another try would be made for her there.

I went over and took her hand. "You feel all right?"

"Yes. Do you . . . have to go?"

"I'll be back." I squeezed her fingers gently. "I'm sorry you were caught in the middle, kid."

She smiled at me, her eyes coming back to life. "I understand."

"Not yet you don't, but let me put it this way. You had basic training with British Intelligence. You were told to expect things like this. You've seen it happen before and now it's happening again. What's going on involves the security of your country and mine both. What happens in the world can hinge on the outcome of this operation. We have a side angle with them making a try for you but it ties in with what they're after. You'll have to stay on your toes. You're cleared to carry a gun if you have to and I want you to keep a rod handy. Your embassy will be notified by now and they'll keep a cover on you as well as me. Later we'll arrange a contact and I may even dangle you as bait if I have to. I don't want to, but I may have to."

"Is it . . . really that big?"

The nylon cord was still on the floor where I dropped it. I picked it up, stretched it out and showed it to her. "These aren't ordinary knots. They're specialty jobs designed for torture, then death. We're playing in a big pro game and any time you forget it take a look at your souvenir." I dropped the nylon in her hand. She fingered it once seriously, then looked up at me again.

"There won't be any forgetting, darling."

I leaned down, kissed her mouth gently, then stood up. Lennie was watching me. "Take good care of her, boy," I said.

"Don't worry."

"I'm not."

Downstairs I found the doorman on the curb, back opening cab doors. When he was alone I said, "Get the lock on Miss Caine's door fixed, will you?"

"I already checked with the maintenance man. He's coming right over."

"Anybody hear the shot?"

"So far nobody complained. You can't hear nuthin' on the other floors and both parties down the other end of the hall are out. Nope, I don't think anybody heard a thing."

"Good. You yell if you see our boy again."

"I'll do better'n that," he told me, bunching the muscles under his coat again. "I don't like my tenants molested."

"Just save a little piece for me," I said.

"Sure. Just a little hunk."

chapter 4

From the hotel I called Newark Control and put my report through. Virgil Adams was on the desk there, got it all down and said, "Want us to start a run on Malcolm Turos?"

"Go ahead. See if you can get him located. He probably came in on a forged passport or through the Cuban screen like they've been doing lately. Any identification on him will be through his voice. This guy can handle a disguise pretty well. You have any photos on him over there?"

"Nothing late and nothing clear. I don't think they'll do you any good."

"Send them over anyway. You might try the Brazilian end. He operated there under the name of Arturo Pensa."

"Isn't that the guy you shot?"

"The same. If he was in a hospital there they might have photos. The local police would have been in on it. Besides, you never can tell what you can find in a newspaper morgue. The place was full of flashbulbs popping that night."

"We'll give it a try."

"Anything new on Teddy?"

"Not a thing. Pete hasn't reached us yet either. Martin Grady's getting a little edgy and you know what that means. If we don't get anything in a couple of days he'll throw a team out. That situation is too touchy to move in on yet so I hope he goes slowly."

"He knows what he's doing."

"Yeah, but with the investigation going he can't afford to lose control. We have a man inside of Interpol and we may come up with something on that end. If Tedesco is still alive and they can reach him they'll break him loose. We can hold any charge they make if we have to as long as they save his skin. I wish you were over there, Tiger."

"So do I."

"Don't lose hope. You might go yet." He paused, said, "Hang on a minute," and after I heard papers shuffling, came back with, "Okay, the action on Turos is started. They're contacting our people now. There's a ten grand going price on his head and we can up it if we have to."

"I'll keep in touch. I still have the feeling he'll make the try for me."

"One word of thought, Tiger."

"What's that?"

"Don't kill him."

I said, "If he has anything to say I'll make him talk first. Don't I always?" Then I hung up.

At a quarter to eight I was at Ernie Bentley's soaking in a tub of dye. I came out of it three shades darker than the tan I already had, and with a hairpiece to fit over the wig, the dark glasses and a native costume I could pass in a crowd for one of the Saudi Arabian boys if nobody looked too closely. Ernie was putting the finishing touches on with makeup when Tom, Dick and Harry came in behind Jack Brant. They weren't wearing their grins any more. Apparently Jack had filled them in pretty good and they knew what was in the wind.

All of them looked at me, the three guys a little dumbstruck, and when I checked myself in a mirror I could see why. Jack shook his head, laughing at me in the glass from behind my shoulder. "Damn, if you don't look like a seventh son. You sure you're *not* a eunuch?"

"I can get affidavits to prove it, buddy."

"Never mind. I can remember a few incidents. . . ."

To shut him up I nudged his gut with my elbow. "Everybody set?"

"Better than you think. Some of the boys on the dock are friends of mine. We're going in unannounced and you'll get first crack like you wanted."

"Every little bit helps."

In a low tone Jack said seriously, "You sure there won't be any trouble? That's the only thing that shook the boys, but one way or another, they're still willing to go along."

"Then they can stop sweating."

"Good enough. Let's go then."

The city is funny. Look normal, get the standoff. Be a little bit different, carry a clipboard, use a gimmick, do anything not normal, and nobody will ask a question. We passed the single police guard covering the side exit when he couldn't understand Harry's polite chatter but didn't want to take the chance of getting involved with possible international diplomacy and its repercussions. We were on the ship before the passenger gangplank was down, through the crowd behind a white-coated steward while the police cordon was being formed on the dock below. Harry's hundred out of my pocket got us straight passage to the luxury suite where the steward knocked gently and the voice behind the door called to come in.

Like chameleons, my three friends changed. They stood there bowing politely while I followed their motions, their soft voices murmuring the amenities of the East, their meaning not quite reaching me. And it happened like I expected it to, the recognition, the taking to the bosom, the almost instant friendship . . . reserved, but pleasant.

Teish El Abin rose from his chair, a small, wiry man apparently in his early sixties, brown as a walnut left over from last season, but with bright snake eyes that could look right through you. He showed his Western indoctrination and shook hands with all of us, turned and introduced us to the taller saturnine man in the closely fitted English-cut suit, and I was the last to shake hands with Sarim Shey.

There was something slimy about this one. He was a little too sincere. He could smile with his mouth and not with his eyes and his hand was that of someone soft only in the palm while the rest of him was hard as nails. I had known killers like that who could wield a knife or trigger a gun with manicured fingers that an hour before and an hour later fondled a woman with never a thought to the interim between or the blood that ran or the voices that screamed.

Sarim Shey was a man to watch closely. His fawning attitude toward Teish was only a guise. He was a power within himself and knew it. His features were fine and sharp, his skin lighter than anyone else's, and his voice had a deliberately cultured British accent. When he walked he had the grace of a cat or a person well trained in the deadly arts of Oriental death.

I knew he was watching me. So was Teish El Abin. They seemed to accept the fact that I was mute from birth because where they came from it wasn't at all uncommon. It was my size they were looking at, my mannerisms, trying to decipher something that was just a little unreal. But my three friends caught it too and carried the play away from me, keeping me in the background while they made the pleasantries.

I knew our time was almost up. Five minutes was as much as we could ask. Then she came in. Nobody had to tell me who she was.

Vey Locca.

You could feel her presence even before you saw her, sense the aroma of musky perfume before you smelled it. Although her eyes never moved she saw everyone at once the way a woman can and above their heads our eyes met briefly before I bowed automatically in the fashion of the others and I knew it was me she was watching.

She wasn't tall, but she gave the appearance of height. Vey Locca was a Eurasian with a proud tilt to her head, hair black as an arctic midnight matching her eyes even to the glints and highlights that shone there. Her mouth was full and luscious, accented by the inherited cheekbones of her forebears. She was a high, full-breasted woman who walked with a deliberate stance that thrust her beauty forward provocatively, each lithe step outlining the youthful swelling of her thighs. Every mannerism seemed to be a combination of the graces of two continents, from the minute finger movements to the demurely subtle facial gestures that made her appear to be both subservient and dominant at the same instant.

Like the men, she held out a delicate hand, clasped each person briefly, and when she came to me lingered just a little longer, ostensibly because of sympathy for my incapacitation. In her own tongue she welcomed me aboard, then, as if it were something offhand, asked if I enjoyed the United States. I caught just enough of it to understand the question, nodded quickly with a smile, took my hand away and made a typical "okay" sign with my thumb and forefinger. The puzzle in her eyes was there and gone almost before it could be recognized, but I caught it all right. Of the three she was the only one who thought me out of place and now she couldn't be sure. She turned away, spoke to the others, then we went through the bows again and left.

As we went out Hal Randolph and four I.A.T.S. men were converging on the corridor, stationing men about quietly. They glanced at us briefly as we passed, but said nothing. Only when we reached the gangplank area did a plainclothesman stop us, but a little bit of gibberish from Harry, broad, friendly smiles and a bow got us waved on impatiently.

We left the same way we came on, were passed through to where Jack waited nervously, shucked our clothes and got back to normal again. We hopped a cab at the corner and I told the driver to take us over to the Blue Ribbon on Forty-fourth Street. I wanted George to take a look at me done up in brown.

It was too early for the lunch crowd to be in, and after a double-take George led us to a table in the back and sent a round of drinks in. Jack said, "Okay, how did it go?"

"I saw what I wanted to see. They're trouble, all right."

"If the customs boys ever find out what we pulled the stink will go pretty high."

"Quit worrying."

"Then what's the next move?"

I nodded toward Harry. "This boy knows his way around. If you can break him loose a few days and I can use him, he might pick up some good bits and pieces. I only catch the loose ends of the language and if they want to converse it will be in their own dialect."

"Interpreter?"

"Just about."

"Won't they know him?"

"I think Ernie can do a reverse job on him that will take. I saw it done before. Either that or we'll pass him off as being from another country."

"Suppose they get wise?"

"Our meeting was pretty damn brief. By now they'll be shaking hands with dozens more and in another day they won't be remembering individuals."

"You hope."

"Put it up to Harry."

Jack grinned at me and waggled a thumb across the table. "I don't have to. Look at his face. He's having a ball."

"Tell me, Harry," I said.

In a surprising Brooklyn accent he said, "The king you met is a cruel man, my friend. He had killed two of my family. The people living under his hand do not live well. I can tell you this . . . whatever he is planning is not for the good of the people, but only for himself. I will do whatever you want because I have learned many things in this country. I know why it is you do the things you do too. It is my desire to help."

"Then you're in, buddy. And thanks."

"I thank *you*, sir," he said seriously.

"Go over and get registered in at the Taft. Your last name's unpronounceable, so use Smith." I handed him a couple of bills across the table and said, "Get yourself a tux and keep it ready and stay there until I contact you."

"Yes, Mr. Tiger."

"One more thing . . . if there's any rough stuff, stay out of it."

"Please . . ."

"What?"

"I am quite capable, sir. I have fought in an army several times."

"This isn't a desert war, feller."

"All killing is alike. It is merely a matter of location and

44

method. I would rather you thought of me as not being helpless."

"You bought it, Harry."

We finished the sandwiches George brought us and split up there. I let them go out first, then followed after I finished my coffee. The noon crowd was just beginning to filter in and I went out through the bar, waving so long to big Jim.

At two-fifteen a messenger service delivered a manila envelope to my hotel. I tipped the boy and went back to look at the photos Virgil Adams sent over. They were eight-by-ten blow-ups of Malcolm Turos but had been taken out of focus with an apparently cheap camera at least ten years ago. In one he was standing outside the stage-door entrance of a theater shaking hands with some admirers, a bouquet of flowers in his hands, an unimposing man in topcoat and homburg with a heavy mustache and a thin smile. The other was a summertime shot taken when he was about to enter a car with a woman. He had no mustache here and wore a light-colored suit. Neither picture could be used for positive identification and unless Virgil came up with something from Brazil I had to rely on the hazy glimpse of the guy going down in front of my gun during the shoot-out there. And all I could recall was an ill-fitting white suit, a floppy panama hat and a nondescript face going down in a heap with the blood spurting from his neck.

I stuck the photos in the bottom of my suitcase, snapped it shut and got into the shower to soak off the stain I had bathed in. By the time I had toweled myself back to normal the phone rang and when I picked it up Charlie Corbinet said, "Smart move, Tiger."

I grinned, but he couldn't see it. "I like to see the face of the enemy."

"You have more than you think. Some of them are domestic."

"Great," I said. "Thanks for the warning, but why?"

"Because some of them are on their way up right now. If you have a rod get it out of sight. They'll pull you in with any excuse right now. Why the hell you register in your own name I'll never know. I thought I taught you better."

"You did, that's why I did it this way. Thanks."

"Get some good lies ready."

"I'm an expert." I hung up quickly, took off the rig with the .45 and looked around for a place to ditch it. I didn't want to lose the piece, not that it couldn't be replaced, but it was fitted to my own hand and sighted in for accuracy, too much a part of me to lose. In this state I wasn't licensed to carry it and they could hit me with a Sullivan charge without even listening to an explanation.

You don't hide guns inside TV sets or air conditioners. These boys would check out every inch of the place, every ledge outside the window, every spot in the bathroom and closet, and unless I figured something out in a hurry I had it.

I opened the window and looked out. Two floors down a spiked iron grillwork divided the terraces between apartments, the grill running up the side of the building, jutting out two feet to discourage access from one side to the other. I took off my belt, strung it through the trigger guard, buckled it and held it out in a wide loop. As the buzzer sounded I dropped it, and for a second, thought I had missed, but the belt caught a spike of the grill and stayed there. I grinned again, lowered the window and went to the door.

Hal Randolph stood there with another big guy, behind them a pair of young, gray-suited guys who could have just come from Madison Avenue. I said, "Come on in, gentlemen."

He put the warrant in my hand first, his mouth forcing a smile of pleasure. "Shakedown, Mann. Hope it doesn't inconvenience you."

"Not a bit. Mind if I finish dressing?"

"You're not going anywhere."

I unfolded the warrant, read it and glanced at him. "Not unless you find what you're looking for."

He didn't have to tell the others what to do. They were pros too, working quickly and smoothly, never missing a bet, hitting the obvious places then moving on to other spots. They laid a box of .45 shells on the bed alongside the leather holster and kept on looking. Hal picked up the box and flipped the top open. "Where's the gun, Tiger?"

"Don't be stupid."

"We're not."

I finished putting on my shirt and tie, buttoning up in front of the mirror. Behind me one of the young guys had the window open and was checking the ledges, feeling for any cords that might be attached to the frame. "No law against carrying cartridges, is there?"

"Unfortunately, no."

They took another ten minutes before they were finished. Everything was back in place, but nobody was satisfied at all. Hal stood there trying to hold his composure, his face dark with suppressed anger. Idly, he picked up the envelope, looked at it and said, "Mind?"

"Be my guest."

When he saw the pictures he knew what he had. He took

them over under the light, studied them carefully, and passed them to the big guy who had come in with him. When he put them back he threw the folder down on the bed. "Want to talk about this, Tiger?"

I shrugged. "Why not?"

"What's your connection with him?"

"I shot him once in Brazil. The slug caught his throat and ruined his lovely baritone and now he'd like to get back at me."

"Go on."

I hooked a chair leg with my toe, pulled it over and sat down. "He's here in the U.S."

"We know. There's no record of his entry."

"Malcolm Turos isn't one to do things the easy way," I smiled.

Hal Randolph and the others exchanged glances, then came back to me, every eye focused on my face. Each one took a position strategically and held it, not knowing what to expect. "Does the warrant include an interrogation?"

"It can be arranged," Hal said casually.

"Don't bother yourself."

"Then let's get back to Turos. I don't think he'd make a specific trip here to nail you."

"What's the answer then?"

"Quit stalling and get to the point. Let's update the talk and put Teish El Abin in the picture. Let's discuss four persons in native dress who got on and off a ship unhampered by police or customs officials."

"How about that?" I said with fake surprise. "Where am I there?"

"That's what I want to know."

"Sorry, buddy."

Hal took a deep breath and looked like he was about to explode. Then he let the air out of his lungs and strode to the window, looked out and down for a moment before turning back to me again. "Three were genuine countrymen of Teish's, all right. The other was out of character. He was a mute and big. He wore dark glasses. He had a physical description that could have been you."

"A lot of guys fit into my suits, mister."

"But there's something that stinks. Of Teish's countrymen, only nine are known to be in the States. They were all checked out and all were too far away to have been on the ship."

"So?"

"That puts somebody else into the picture. We know about Tedesco being in Selachin and what happened there. You're involved up to your ears so quit playing games."

I stopped smiling at him and leaned forward in the chair. "Okay, Hal, then I'll lay it on the line for you. Maybe you don't like our operation and I don't give a damn, but we've come up with the answers when you couldn't. The last time out I let myself be a target at your suggestion and we all got what we went after. Maybe the routine wasn't what you would have liked, but it worked. I'll go along with any of you any time and have most of the time. Outside the country we're all even, but here you have the edge and you throw the heat at me. Okay, you can make it rough, but I can make it easy."

"Spell it out, Tiger."

"Get me a clearance on that gun again."

"It can't be done."

I leaned back in the chair again and sat there a few seconds. "No?"

One of the young guys said, "It can be worked through Army Intelligence."

Hal glared at him, his teeth tight. Finally he walked to the phone, dialed a number, and spoke softly a few minutes before hanging up. "They want your old ASN, the serial numbers on the gun and your 201 file."

"At Church Street?"

"Yes."

"They'll get it in the morning." I got up and handed Hal Randolph a pen and sheet of paper. "Certify the deal in writing."

"It won't mean a thing."

"Then don't fight it. Just do it."

He wrote a few paragraphs, signed it and handed it to me. I gave the pen and paper to each one in turn, had them witness it, took it back and folded it into my pocket. The last guy said pleasantly, "One thing, Mann . . ."

"I know," I cut in, "where's the gun?"

"A matter of professional interest."

I showed them and they stored the gimmick away in their minds before they left. At the door Hal said, "I'll be in touch with you."

"Do that," I told him.

Then I made arrangements with Central to get my papers to Army Intelligence and went down and got my rod back. I felt better with it back at my waist again.

Rondine took her lunch break from one to two, so I gave her the extra hour so I'd catch her at the U.N. and got the call through at three sharp. I knew Lennie Byrnes would be monitoring her calls for her and he gave me the clear sign and put her on. So far neither of them had seen anyone out of the ordinary nor was any overt move made against them. Lennie was staying in tight, ready for any emergency, acting the role of a magazine writer doing a piece on U.N. translators. Everyone had been very cooperative.

I told them I'd pick them up outside the building at six and if I wasn't there to get right back to the apartment and stay there. I hung up and was about to dial Charlie to tell him what went on with Hal Randolph when the phone went off.

I said, "Yes?"

"Virgil Adams, Tiger. Identify."

Two words made the contact definite and he said, "Telephoto just arrived from Brazil. Your tip about the hospitals having photos paid off. We have a set of three, but two are of the wound, only one gives a good, clear close-up of his face. I'll send it over by messenger right away."

"Okay, but get it to Ernie Bentley. I'll want some dupes and I don't want anything put in my box downstairs."

"Roger. Be about an hour."

"How about the informants?"

"Nothing. We've covering the usual spots, but I don't have any feeling that we'll luck out there. Turos knows the ropes too well. If this is a solo operation on his part he won't make any contacts at all."

"He already made one," I reminded him.

"That may be all you'll need."

"I hope not. Reach me through Ernie later if anything develops."

"Roger."

I hung up, tried Charlie Corbinet but got no answer. Now I had to start playing it right down the line again.

chapter 5

You take all your Federal agencies, your highly trained but obscure intelligence units, your college degrees and your high IQ, hand-selected personnel working under bureau orders, sure, you take them. When you want a job done, give me New York's finest in or out of uniform. Give me the beat cop, the plainclothesmen, the dedicated people so imbued with the city and its environs that they can do a character study of anybody in a half second.

They came out of the womb of the city and although they're tied to her apron strings by a paycheck, they're the big independents who love her enough to keep her clean. They sweat in the sun at street crossings, they prowl the festered parts of her body because she nursed them in the beginning, they take the abuse of the other sons and never quit. Even when you find a bad one or one on the take, he's still a guy ready to lay his life on the line if he has to and will go in a dark alley after a killer with no concern about his own safety. But most are the best. They have to be or they wouldn't be there.

These are the ones who can analyze the population at a glance. They can spot a stranger, single out the wrong characters, sense the mood of the city and prepare in advance for what will happen. These are the crime surgeons, the crime deterrents, the ones who answer when you yell for a cop.

I called Dick Gallagher at his precinct number hoping to get a lead on the way the department was going to handle Teish El Abin's visit to the city and for the first time I ran into luck. Over coffee at the hash house opposite the station Dick told me his vacation had just been stepped up a week and he was burning about it. He had to cancel his reservations at Atlantic

City and nothing was vacant when he got his leave.

"Why?" I asked him.

"Visiting dignitaries. You read about our new friends from Selachin?"

"Who hasn't?"

"So we're covering His Highness. What with the World's Fair, the race riots and the usual summer trouble we're the only section they can draw from for special duty and I get tapped."

"Maybe there'll be some excitement."

"How? By playing doorman at a reception?"

"Who are you alerted for?"

"The usual fanatics," he shrugged. "These Middle East characters can raise some powerful hatreds. Look what happens with the S.A. bunch. Double it and you get this outfit. It's like having Nasser around . . . you never know what side is going to start shooting first and we're always caught in the middle."

"What is it, invitation only?"

"Damn right."

"Sounds interesting. Maybe I can wangle a card?"

"Why?"

I grinned at him and finished my coffee. "I know a few editors who would print the story. I hear he's got a nice chick with him."

"Nice trouble. I haven't seen one yet who couldn't make it."

"How can I get in, Dick?"

"You can't, old buddy. Every invitation is numbered and will be checked off against a master list."

"Who holds that?"

"Now do you think the Washington boys would trust us with a thing like that? Hell, one of their men will handle it. Besides, where do you fit in? I didn't think you went the social route."

"Politics intrigue me," I said.

"Yeah, sure. Me too. You go for cocktails, pink sandwiches, limp handshakes and double talk. Baloney. Besides, you know the big deal at the reception?"

I shook my head.

Dick said, "Teish El Abin gets to see himself on TV for the first time. They're broadcasting his five-minute speech to the welcoming committee on the news program then slamming in a closed-circuit segment for twenty minutes covering his whole arrival. Nobody gets to see it but the bunch at the reception. A phoney deal, but it's got him happy. The networks wouldn't touch the idea so they're doing it this way."

"Fast thinking. Whose idea was it?"

"Sergeant Anderson's, down at the 4th Precinct. You can't imagine the State Department dreaming that one up, could you?"

"Their dreams aren't so realistic. Look, I'm going to try to wangle an invitation."

"Don't waste your time."

"I won't," I said. "By the way, you ever heard of Malcolm Turos?"

He gave me a funny little smile that could mean anything. Finally he said, "You're not paying off to receive official information, are you?"

"I don't have to."

"Yeah, I heard of him."

"Just lately," I grinned.

He didn't have to be on guard with me and knew it. "Very lately. His description has been flashed to all departments."

"It won't fit any more," I told him.

He waited for the rest, never losing his grin. "No?"

"Like a nice clear picture of the guy, a late photo you can use?"

"When?"

"Maybe I'll deliver it tonight."

"No games, Tiger," he said.

"Authenticated. Positive description. If you like I can get you three witnesses to prove the point."

Dick leaned forward staring at me, his face serious. "I'll take that, Tiger buddy. I'll assume you know the details of what you're intimating so I won't have to spell it out for you."

"I do."

"Okay, then we can get it circulated and throw out a net. This guy is top priority on the wanted sheet and if you come across with a bit like that maybe we can nail him. They suspect he's in this area and are putting out directives on the hour. Washington's got their best men in to work with us but we haven't got a decent thing to go on."

"You will have."

"I'll be waiting."

We finished another coffee before we left and I let Dick drive me down a couple of blocks from Ernie Bentley's place, then walked the rest of the way. Virgil Adams had delivered the photo of Turos from Brazil and Ernie had a dozen duplicates ready for me in a manila folder.

Fifteen minutes after I called him, little Harry was there getting a chemical treatment from Ernie that toned up his swarthy skin complexion, and in a dark suit, his hair reshaped and a thin mustache added, he was far from the turbaned and robed native that was on the *Queen* with me. Just to make sure he wouldn't be tempted into exposing hidden animosities against a king who killed off some of his family, I patted him down, took a slim knife out of his sleeve and left it with Ernie. Harry grinned sheepishly, but said nothing, then went over with me to the hotel where I got dressed for the occasion.

The Stacy was one of the newer hotels, towering and massive, like a new tombstone in an old graveyard. It nestled in the center of Manhattan defiantly, a new big kid who pushed out the older residents and dared them to do anything about it. Limousines were nose to bumper in the no parking zones, all sporting DPL tags that meant diplomatic immunity to police citations and cabs were disgorging the pompous and the famous like sick cats. Each side of the street was lined with uniformed patrolmen and a dozen mounted sergeants walked their horses along the curb to keep things moving, with a few motorcycle cops standing by for anything that might develop. The gawking crowd attracted by the display was probably loaded with plainclothesmen, but I only spotted a couple I knew by sight.

Anybody entering the lobby was directed either to one side or another, those attending the reception to the left, the rest shunted the opposite way. A red velvet rope with matching carpet led the way to the first door where a pair of smiling young men in tuxedos inspected the invitations, tore a corner off the card to see if they were genuine, with a colored thin inner layer, then passed you inside to go through another screening.

Washington was playing this one close to their vests, not taking any chances at all. I didn't bother with trying to force the issue. With Harry beside me I made the rounds of the lobby, found the pay phones, then went in and called the desk. The harried operator put me through to the clerk and when I asked to speak to the nearest uniformed patrolman he almost choked up. Through the glass door I could see him wave a cop over and put him on.

He said, "Patrolman Delaney speaking. Who is this?"

"My name is Mann. I have a package for Lieutenant Gallagher he's expecting. How the hell can I get it to him?"

"He's on duty right now and . . ."

"I know he is, but he wants this. Can you get him out in the lobby long enough to pick it up? This is department business, not personal and he'd appreciate it."

That much decided him. He said he would give him the message and I told him I'd be at the desk in a few minutes. Instead of waiting, I hung up when the cop did, nodded for Harry to follow me, and trailed the policeman to the other side of the room and waited while he spoke to a plainclothes guard and disappeared in a room.

He didn't take long. Dick was right behind him and when he saw me, waved for me to join him. The guard frowned, let us pass inside and I handed the folder over to Dick. "Here's your boy Malcolm Turos."

He pulled out the photos, scanned the information sheet Ernie had clipped to the top one, and grinned. "Let me get these over to the office. I'll have one of my men rush it. Tell me something . . . do the Feds have copies?"

"Not yet they don't."

"This ought to shake them a little bit."

"Now a favor . . ."

"Yeah, I know. You want to meet royalty. If you get the bum's rush, think up a good lie. There's a service entrance one reporter already crashed so you can keep me off the hook if you can make it stick. From now on I don't even know you." He looked at Harry a second and added, "Your friend okay?"

"He wouldn't be here if he wasn't."

"Your funeral, Tiger." We made a circuitous route around the main section, went in a side door, and there we were with the political wheels nice and painlessly. So far, at least.

Most of the crowd was grouped at the other end of the room, separating, gradually, into smaller huddles of four and five, plying the trade in international diplomacy already, smiles as bland and false as a snake's, cocktail glasses in their hands to disguise the fact that it was anything but an affair of state.

Apparently the reception line had been run and the formal part was over. It was time for pleasantries and subtleties, and in a mob like this one, anything could happen. I told Harry to grab a glass and circulate, but to stay close to Teish or Sarim Shey whom I could see occupying a corner, carrying on an animated conversation with a half dozen dignitaries. Vey Locca was about ten feet away, surrounded by fascinated men of varied ages totally captivated by this charming Oriental broad. Just thinking of her bedding down with Teish was an ugly thought, but in the world of power and money, some women would do anything.

The latecomers were still being passed through the one door and it was this bunch I picked to follow into the main grouping, trying to figure out a way to get close to the guests of honor without being obstrusive. I knew damn well the place would be loaded with agents and enough knew me by sight to make it rough if I were spotted, so I had to go along on luck. One advantage I had was that I was *there,* so they'd have to assume I was cleared through by some other authority.

Two of the new arrivals were on the Senate Foreign Relations Committee followed by a Midwestern senator and a New York councilman. I knew them all and turned aside until they passed. Behind them a distinguished type on the portly side with a square-cut beard and bristling mustache minced along, then a few from the U.N. I had seen over there stepped in. I dropped right in behind them.

I thought I had it made until a finger tapped my shoulder and an Oxford-accented voice said, "I say, old boy, you certainly get around, don't you?"

I grinned and moved my hand away from the .45. I said, "Talbot, you can get yourself killed awfully fast that way."

"Oh, I don't think you're the type to go for a public display of that sort, now are you?"

"You'd be surprised." I looked at him squarely. "So what's your angle, kid? One word from you and I'm on my ear."

Talbot smiled nicely and patted my arm. "No necessity for that sort of thing."

"You've been detailed to cover me, haven't you?"

"Along with several others, though I didn't imagine I'd find you here. Really, you're leading our chaps an amusing race. How do you do it?"

"It isn't easy."

"Well now. Let's make it that way. Since I can keep you well under surveillance as long as we're together I think it might be better if I simply played your game and sort of watched out for things, don't you think?"

"Don't do me any favors."

He laughed, then steered me toward the corner where Teish El Abin was holding court. Vey Locca was beside him now, and the court was more hers than his. "I'm here by special invitation, you know," Talbot told me. "Several years ago I spent some time in Selachin at the request of Her Majesty and knew old Teish on a rather personal level. Seems like he took a fancy to one of our nationals and induced her into his domain for certain earthy relationships, and when her family objected I was selected to, er . . . induce her out again."

"You mean ransom."

"Ugly word. Doesn't fit modern diplomacy at all. However, her family was quite wealthy and a simple trade was effected. The king and I got to be rather good friends after that. Seems I hit the nail on the head when he desired a present in return for her services."

"What was it?"

"You'd never believe it."

"Try me."

"Along with the cash settlement he tended to ignore since there was little to buy with money, a 16mm projector and a trunk full of rather risqué films did the trick. The old boy's quite a lecher, you know. Why he'd settle for movies when the real things were on hand for actual performances, I don't understand, but all of us have our peculiarities, I guess."

"What's yours?"

"I'm the playboy type," he smiled. "Dashing, clever, all that sort of thing. Really interesting hobby if you can afford to pursue it. Surprising results sometime. I'm thinking of writing a book one day."

"Sell it to Teish. He'd enjoy it."

Talbot looked at me indignantly. "My book will be more of a clinical study of the subject. Nothing vulgar. Now, if *you* were to do an autobiography . . ."

"I haven't lived long enough to write one yet."

He grinned again, then led me through the crowd to Teish El Abin. In a business suit he seemed even smaller than before, older, but there was still that crafty face and the eyes that ran ahead of his thoughts, probing their way into new fields of power he could already taste. The bond between him and Talbot was evident, two men sharing a common knowledge, and Teish shook his hand warmly. Somewhere along the line Teish had picked up a conversational command of English accented with overtones of his native tongue, but beside him Vey Locca spoke almost flawlessly to a heavyset American and even above her voice I could hear that of Sarim Shey whose tone and vernacular almost matched that of Talbot's.

When the two of them finished a minute's reminiscing, shared a low joke and chuckled over something out of the past, Talbot pulled me forward and said, "May I introduce my good friend, Mr. Mann."

I knew that crazy Talbot was enjoying my hesitation as I tried to find the right words, but the king saved the situation by saying, "Ah, yes. It is very nice, and please, you may just call me Teish. In my country it is not only a name, but a title and there is no disrespect. After all, your Biblical characters had no last names now, did they? And were not Abraham and Moses great leaders?"

I grabbed his hand, shook it briefly and smiled. "Thank you, sir. I hope you're enjoying your stay."

Teish nodded and glanced around him briefly. "I anticipate a fine visit." Then his eyes seemed to take me in all at once, his mind trying to find a slot to put me in. "Have we met before?"

Talbot said, "My friend here is one of those wealthy American industrialists who collects money. Always lobbying in

Washington to try to keep some of it."

Teish looked interested when the dollar was mentioned. "Oh, and what business are you in, please?"

"Oil," I lied. "Research and development. I have quite an extensive operation."

Momentarily, I felt Talbot's fingers tighten on my arm. He threw me a lead unwittingly and I grabbed hold for all it was worth. Talbot knew the score as well as I did, but anybody can make a mistake and he made his. I had the ball now and he realized I took it away from him. The light in Teish's eyes was even brighter than when the money was mentioned.

He seemed to twinkle a bit and said, "Very nice. Perhaps we may have a little time to talk later. May I ask the name of your company?"

And now I stuck it in and broke it off. Martin Grady's syndicate had the controlling interest in the new giant that was emerging on the scene in the oil industry with patents that had some of the older established outfits squirming. I'd be backed up to the hilt in this one and I knew it, so I could play it like an end taking a clean pass from the quarterback and with a little broken field running I could be in the end zone.

"AmPet Corporation. We're rather new, but . . ."

"Ah," Teish interrupted, "but not unknown. Yes, I have heard of AmPet." He stopped his visual interrogation of me then, completely intrigued by the thought of oil and the value of AmPet. Apparently the old boy had done plenty of research before he left Selachin for the States. He turned, took Vey Locca's arm, disengaging her from her admirers with a friendly apology and said, "May I introduce Mr. Mann, my dear. He is an owner of AmPet Corporation of which we have heard so much lately." He smiled at me as she held out her hand. "Vey Locca," he said, "my betrothed. We are to be married shortly."

Her hand was warm and firm in mine. "You are very fortunate," I told him.

"Yes," he said, his eyes going up to hers. "We will have many sons. In my country that is of great importance."

"It is here too," I said.

Somehow Vey Locca seemed as perceptive as Teish was, smiling and friendly, but strangely puzzled when she looked at me. "How nice to see you, Mr. Mann. I have the feeling we've met before."

"I wish I could have had the pleasure, but I'm afraid not."

Very gently she squeezed my hand. Nobody could see it, but I could feel the sensual pressure she put there. Her eyes had a smile of their own, a hint of anticipation and I could almost feel the warmth of her penetrating across the short space that separated us. I let her hand go, conscious of a movement to my left.

Vey Locca waved casually and said, "Sarim Shey, Mr. Mann. Our adviser."

He held out his hand and shook mine with a typically European gesture. "Charmed," Sarim Shey said, then smiled at Talbot. He held his hand out to him then. "Ah, Mr. Talbot. I have heard so much about you. Funny we haven't met before. Same school and all, y'know."

"Large place, Oxford," Talbot told him. "Believe I was ahead of you." It only took Talbot a second to provide the interference I needed. He had Sarim Shey to one side rehashing the old days and left me alone, but close enough where I could see him. Out of the corner of my eye I saw Harry moving in, talking earnestly to the guy with the thick beard and mustache and a tall bald-headed man I had seen around the U.N. who never went anywhere without a rosette in his lapel and several miniature decorations pinned to his chest.

I was about to throw out a feeler for conversation when Teish did it for me. He suddenly looked at his watch, then broke into a wrinkled smile. "If you'll pardon me . . . there is a news broadcast I would like to see."

"Certainly," I said.

"But please join us, Mr. Mann. There is a television ready in the anteroom next door. I . . . must admit to vanity, I'm afraid. They are showing my picture. Do you mind?"

Vey Locca smiled and took my arm. "I'm sure he will be pleased."

"My pleasure," I said. I looked around. "Is everyone invited?"

"No, just a few. It is not a very big room." She glanced over her shoulder and said, "Sarim . . . Mr. Talbot, we are ready."

About twenty of the few hundred present were admitted inside. Those who were lucky enough not to be invited didn't seem displeased—there were too many waiters with trays loaded with martinis and Manhattans and the day was just beginning for them. Little Harry was more astute than I thought. Somehow he had gotten in with his two companions and was at the rear of the pack trying to look over heads at the TV.

Only one chair was provided, and Teish El Abin sat in it directly in front of the set the way a kid would, squirming eagerly. Vey Locca was on one side, me directly behind her, with Sarim Shey doing the honors of tuning in the news broadcast.

We watched the commercial, then the announcer, and somehow the Washington influence made itself felt because Teish was the first one he mentioned who would be seen right after an important message from the sponsor.

It would have been great, but something started happening to the set. It began to snow, then fuzz out and while Teish let out a little squeal of dismay and a hum went around the room, one of the young guys in a dark business suit who had all the earmarks of an agency man picked up a phone and called the maintenance department. He wasn't taking any chances on fouling up the guest of honor and was right on the ball. I looked at my watch. A commercial and a little chatter from the announcer before they ran the news film would take about a minute and a half and I hoped somebody was smart enough to anticipate trouble and have another set or a repair man standing by.

Vey Locca looked back at me anxiously and said, "Oh, I hope there won't be trouble. He wanted so badly to see the program."

I winked at her. "No sweat. They'll have a special rerun if it goes off."

"But it won't be the same," she argued.

She didn't know that the whole phoney deal was already rigged with a closed-circuit setup downstairs to feed Teish's ego on top of his news spot and I wasn't about to mention it. I looked at my watch again. The seconds were ticking off and everybody was murmuring sympathetically. Teish was trying to get Sarim Shey to clear the set, but although he began picking up a Boston station, none of the New York channels were coming in.

I didn't like it a bit. There was something there that didn't look right and I couldn't put my finger on it. Then someone called out from the back and the crowd parted to let a coveralled man through carrying a standard tool kit, urging him to hurry.

He was a small guy in his late forties, taking impatient crabwise steps to get through the mob, walking directly toward us. He seemed constantly to edge around the right of anyone in front of him until he reached me, and when Vey Locca and I stepped aside he would have passed right beside Teish.

I got it then, all right. I gave her a shove that sent her stumbling into a man's arms, a look of sudden fright on her face. I grabbed the guy as he reached Teish, slammed a hand across his ear from behind just as he was reaching and I saw a needle slither from his fingers as he went down with a startled yelp. Teish turned, frozen, one hand going out to protect himself.

The damn crowd was too much. They moved like one person and I went off balance. The guy on the floor scrambled to his feet and shot through the crowd like an animal and nobody seemed to know what was happening. I saw the action as a few assigned to protect Teish closed in, reaching predesignated positions, but even they couldn't get a clean look. I was six feet behind the guy, clawing my way through immobilized bodies, swearing all the way, knowing the guy would make the door if I didn't reach him.

I saw Harry and his two friends and it was the one with the beard who seemed able to comprehend the situation and act on it. He took what looked like a clumsy swipe at the guy with one fist, connected, and the guy fell. I was on him in a second, pinning him there, but he wasn't making any move to get away. Two pair of hands lifted me off him as the agency guys took over, cuffing limp hands behind his back, patting him down for any weapons. In five seconds they had him out the door and I forced my way back to Teish.

He, Vey Locca and Sarim Shey were together covered by two more of the young guys and they made no bones about it because they each had police service revolvers in their hands. Talbot was there, eyes narrowed now, looking for me, waiting for an explanation. I pointed under Teish's chair, reached down and picked up a sliver of wood no longer than a matchstick that had an eighth of an inch of needle protruding from one end.

I handed it to him. "Get this analyzed right away. Ten to one it's got a slow-acting poison on it that would take effect in about fifteen minutes."

Teish's eyes were staring now, frightened. "Please, Mr. Mann . . ."

"No trouble, it's cleared now." I pointed to the TV set. "Can I check something?"

One of the guards there started to say something, but Talbot waved them off, having already established his authority over theirs. "Go ahead, old chap."

I walked over, put the set on the right channel and there was Teish giving the end of his speech to the welcoming crowd at the ship. I knew how they worked it then. I looked at Teish and said, "I'll be back. Come on, Talbot."

They tried to stop us at the door, but Talbot flashed his credentials and got us out. In the corridor I saw Dick Gallagher and he was blazing mad, repositioning his men and throwing out the orders. I yelled to him to follow me and he came running. When we reached the end I said, "No questions, buddy. How do we get to the roof?"

He was sharp enough to wait me out. He pointed, led the

way to the fire exit and we took the stairs two at a time to the top, then went past the two uniformed cops there to the door that led outside. I found the antenna that had been turned, a pipe wrench still fastened to it, but nobody was in sight.

"All the exits covered?"

Dick nodded.

"Then they had him planted here in plenty of time. He's still got to be around."

"Come on, come on. Let's have it."

"They had it timed just right. They screwed up the set downstairs by turning the antenna and fading out the picture, knowing somebody would call a maintenance man in. The guy was supposed to brush past Teish, hit him with the needle and he hardly would have felt it. A little fiddling with the set, then the guy on the roof redirected the antenna to bring in the picture while the maintenance man made his escape. Meanwhile, Teish is sitting there dying and never knowing it."

Dick scanned the rooftop. He had to be there. No other roofs joined this building so he was behind one of the roof exits or the ventilators. We would spread out, each taking a different route to cover any possible escape.

It was Talbot who spotted him behind the enormous air conditioning exhaust structure in the middle of the roof. He let out a shout, pointed and we ran up to cover it from three sides, not knowing if the guy had a gun or not. He took a look to see where we were, the top of his head showing through some latticework on the structure. Dick fired into the air just once, but it was enough. He must have thought we were there to kill and let out a muffled scream and ran like a scared rabbit toward one of the roof doors, then saw us coming and changed direction.

He did it too fast and was too near the edge. The gravel surface of the roof was like marbles under his shoes and he skidded in a frenzied slide toward the top of the parapet, clutching wildly at the air, grabbing momentarily at the slick tiles that covered the raised brick parapet, then his own momentum took him over. We could still hear him screaming ten floors down before he became a dark blob on the sidewalk below that gradually began to glisten a wet red in the lights.

Dick muttered, "Damn!" and put his gun back slowly, then turned toward the exit we came out of.

They had cleared the main room when we got back. The herd had been gathered in another place and only a handful of people were left. Teish, Vey and Sarim were engaged with three people and the largest was Hal Randolph. He followed Teish's eyes, saw me and excused himself. When he reached me there was a florid tone to his skin and he was holding himself in check tightly. "You have some talking to do, Tiger."

"Why?"

"No gas, let's us just talk."

I shrugged. "So I crashed the party. I think you have everything by now."

"Not the little ends that are so important."

I waved my thumb at Talbot. "He'll fill you in. I gave him the needle that was supposed to drop off Teish."

Randolph squinted, looked at Talbot and said, "Well?"

Talbot took his handkerchief out and unfolded it. The gimmick lay in the middle, the tip still dark with a strange substance. "Going over to the lab now. Unless you want to handle it."

Randolph took the handkerchief out of his hand. "I do," he told him, then listened while Talbot filled him in. When he finished, Randolph said, "Come over here." He walked across the room to the other one where the TV set had been installed, pushing the door open. Inside, a table had been pulled up and two men bent over a body stretched out there. "We brought him back in here for a preliminary exam."

I took a look at the body in the coveralls. "That's the one who tried for Teish," I said. "What happened?"

"Look at his neck."

I saw the mark then, a discoloration that seemed to dent in the neck as if somebody had laid a pipe across it. I touched the crease, felt what had happened, then straightened up. "A professional touch. I only knew two people who could pull that trick and both of them are dead now."

"He was dead when our men picked him up. They thought he was unconscious, but that blow was as expertly delivered as a headsman's ax."

I let my mind drift back. "It looked like he just took a swipe at him enough to knock him down."

"Who, Tiger?"

"The guy with the beard." I watched Randolph closely and saw how he was watching me, taking in every inflection of my voice, every gesture I made. "Didn't you pick him up?"

"In the general commotion he seems to have disappeared."

"So why worry? He won't be hard to recognize. Hell, he came in with a card. I saw the guard pick it up at the door."

"Oh, he did that, all right, but the card wasn't his. It belonged to Carmen Beship who had a general resemblance and sported a beard like that, but five minutes ago the eminent Mr. Beship was reported dead in his own apartment from a blow exactly like this guy got." He locked his hands behind his back and rocked on his heels. "And you seem to have taken charge nicely, even to the one on the roof. Nobody's around who can talk, or maybe *you* have an explanation, Tiger?"

He picked one with a beard to cover that bullet scar in his throat. For a guy like him it wouldn't have been hard to locate an invitation list and select the one he wanted. Padding under his clothes would fill him out and he could move in a crowd because you can get lost in one. He had to be on hand in case something went wrong, and when it did he was able to silence the one person who might possibly provide a lead to him. He knew the confusion of the moment would provide a cover for a getaway and used it perfectly. The guy on the roof he wouldn't worry about because that contact would be too vague, and if it wasn't he still wouldn't worry because by now everybody would know of his death on the street outside.

"Malcolm Turos," I said.

"And nobody really knows what he looks like."

I let him see the teeth under my grin. "They do now." I reached in my pocket and handed him one of the duplicate photos I had there. "By now the city police already have it on the wires."

"You bastard!" He grabbed the photo and looked at it closely.

"Why does everybody always call me that?" I asked him.

Dick Gallagher pushed the door open before he could answer me and said, "You're wanted outside here, Tiger."

"He's not going any place," Randolph snarled.

"Then you'd better check with somebody further up. Teish El Abin's asking for him personally and if you don't get the message it's your skin."

I grinned at Randolph who stood there, his face getting redder. "I want to see you later, Mann. Our office. You be there."

"Sure," I said. "You have a paper for me I want to pick up. A gun clearance."

Although nobody had given old Teish the total picture, he put enough of the pieces together himself to know what happened. He was going to get the story anyway so I just gave it to him straight and watched his face tighten into fine lines that highlighted all the thoughts of vengeance that danced in his eyes and when I was done he nodded slowly, waited until he was composed and said quietly, "My most sincere appreciation, Mr. Mann. It will be repaid."

"No necessity for that."

Sarim Shey seemed relieved at my gesture. "I say, you acted so quickly no one really knew what happened. Did you actually *see* the needle he had?"

"Not until he dropped it. But it was all too pat. I caught the angle in time and knew something was coming off."

"Unusual for a . . . businessman to react so quickly, isn't it?" He said it pleasantly enough, but there was more behind it than that. So I leaned heavy on the movie version of the American type and laughed it off. "Not in *my* business," I told him. "Scrambling for bucks is a dogfight every day. I've lived with too many people out for my dough and my skin too damn long not to recognize the signs of something coming off." I stopped, then turned to Teish. "You got any idea who'd pull a stunt like this?"

His smile was expressionless. "One makes many enemies."

"This was organized."

"As are my enemies," he insisted. "It will take a little time to determine which one is responsible. Then countermeasures will be prepared."

"The cops will handle it." I tried to sound offhand and hoped it worked.

His eyes seemed amused at the thought. "Yes," he answered, "I'm sure they will. Now, may I impose upon you for another favor?"

"Any time."

"Sarim and I must attend a conference, a very important matter that concerns our respective governments. In view of . . . what has happened, I do not wish to leave Vey alone." He reached out, took her hand paternally, and smiled. "Would it be asking too much of you to see to her safety until we are free?"

Once again I caught a peculiar sense of emotion that came from Sarim Shey. He stood there, in all respects agreeing with his king, but the act just didn't come across right. I played the game again. "If you'd rather, I'll get Talbot since you and he . . "

"I'd prefer to ask you, Mr. Mann."

I grinned at Vey Locca and nodded. "Be glad to. I just hope there will be no interference from the security personnel. They seem to have everything locked up tight."

"I will see to that, Mr. Mann." He glanced past me, waved a finger at Hal Randolph who was watching us from the door of the other room, called him over and explained briefly what he wanted. I thought Randolph would pop his buttons, but he made a stiff half bow acknowledging the situation and went right along.

Hell, he had to.

We waited until Teish and Sarim had been escorted from the room before we left. I found Vey Locca's mink stole and draped it around her shoulders, letting the back of my fingers deliberately brush against her bare skin. I saw little muscles

64

appear a moment, a small shudder ran through her and she turned her head and looked across her shoulder. "You are a very interesting person, Mr. Mann."

"Nothing special."

A slow smile flitted across her mouth. "And what may I call you?"

"Tiger." When she raised her eyebrows, I added, "It's my name."

I felt her hand slip into mine, her fingers doing strange things. "In my country they tell a story about certain instincts of the tiger."

"I'll have to hear it," I said.

"Yes, you will. Later you will. Now you may take me down to my room and I will expect you to pick me up at eight o'clock. You will be prompt?"

"When one tiger calls another comes running," I said. "They have certain instincts."

She crowded me enough so I could feel the pressure of her breast against my arm. "Perhaps you have heard the story already."

"I wouldn't be a bit surprised."

chapter 6

I called Martin Grady directly as soon as I reached the street. I let him have my report and gave him the pitch on AmPet Corporation. To expedite matters he was turning over a major block of his stock to me until the assignment was completed, when it would be returned. Meanwhile, I'd be listed as a VIP with the outfit in case anybody investigated.

I said, "Well look, I can handle myself in conversation with the general details of oil exploration and refining, but supposing somebody gets specific about the AmPet operation."

Grady grunted and I heard a cigarette lighter flick on. "I just anticipated that. Walter Milos, one of our lab men, is in New York right now. We'll call him from here and have him brief you on the layout. You're a quick study so pack it in. There will be some truth there to fool anybody familiar with our processes, but nothing specific enough to give them a lead to the actual formula. Besides, what you don't know you can't reveal and anybody probing with leading questions will only surmise that you're not giving anything away free."

"Where do we meet?"

"He'll be in another of our suites in the Calvin where Lennie is staying. He checks out tonight so get with it."

"Roger. How's the investigation proceeding?"

Martin Grady chuckled, something I hadn't heard him do in a long time. "Getting nowhere fast. They're trying for any low blow, even to ringing in the tax men, but it pays to be honest. They picked up Steuben and Les to interrogate them on the Miller affair but their alibis held."

"Hell, they only set Miller up. One of their own men knocked him off. They should have been grateful."

"Not those boys. What they want is our leads to their information. Chet passed the word that you're on their list too, so walk softly if you can. Don't think Hal Randolph is the friendly type. He'll go along far enough to drop a noose over your head."

It was my turn to laugh. Randolph had been trying it for a long time but the knot kept coming untied. "No sweat there. Randolph has to go by the book and when a page is torn out he can't move. I'll report through Newark Control later. Anything you think I should know?"

"It's your project, Tiger. You're getting too old to advise any more."

"Thanks a bunch," I said. "I'm still waiting for word on Pete Moore."

"Hang on a minute." Somebody else had come into the office and I heard a few muffled words and the soft rustle of papers. When Grady came back on again he laid out the Selachin situation as briefly as he could.

So far Pete Moore had not made contact with our people in Selachin, but rumors were out already about some peculiar business in the area and behind the Iron Curtain there was a lot of consternation in Soviet circles that had a hand in the project. As for Teddy Tedesco, there was no word. We were going to have to wait until Moore located him.

When I hung up I flagged a cab and had the driver take me to the Taft. I took the elevator up to Harry's room, tapped on his door and called out that it was me. Still cautious, he opened the door on the chain first before he was satisfied and let me in. He still hadn't gotten over the shakes and grinned sheepishly when I noticed it.

"It was not the excitement, sir," he told me. "It was the worry that I would be caught, then I would be back in the desert and soon thereafter my head would be off."

"You're out of it now," I reassured him. "Look, you were with that guy in the beard that belted the TV man."

"Yes. From when he came in."

"Notice anything about him?"

"He was not American. His voice . . . it was very strange."

"The tone or the dialect?"

Harry studied the ceiling a second, thinking. "Mostly his voice. Maybe he . . . he had a cold?"

"He had a hole in his throat I put there once. What did you talk about?"

"Trifles. We discussed the beauty of the lady Vey Locca, the emergence of the lesser kingdoms into national prominence, the war in Viet Nam, but that was all." He walked to the window, looked out, then turned around. "He knew when Teish would be leaving the main room. He was right there to go in, but he did not wish to go to the front. Neither did I, so the arrangement was satisfactory."

"Any talk about himself?"

"None." Harry paused and reconsidered. "Once he commented that he did not like New York. He abhorred the odor of *litchi nuts*. I did not understand."

"A Chinese delicacy," I explained. "They used to have bowls of them in Chinese laundries for the customers. That was all?"

"It was not talk to think upon, sir. It was . . . nothing talk."

"He knew what he was doing."

"But I heard more," Harry offered. "It was after the . . . the event. I was pushed to one side and was close to Teish and Sarim Shey when they were talking. The excitement was too great for Teish and Vey Locca gave him a pill. It was I who brought the water and at that time Sarim Shey was telling him that it was an American plot to kill him so that they could install their own king in Selachin. He was very insistent and Teish was inclined to listen."

"They didn't spot you, did they?"

"It is inconceivable that one would understand our language. No, they made no attempt to hide what they were saying. Yes, there was one other thing . . . Teish was pleased with you. I don't think he really wanted to believe what Sarim Shey was telling him."

I perched on the edge of the table and thought about it. Even if Teish didn't believe it, Sarim could make it look plausible, an American assassination attempt stopped by an American deliberately to make it look as if it had come from another direction. Men were expendable and there was nobody to prove otherwise. It had happened like that before when the stakes were big enough.

I said, "Okay, Harry, you did your job. Sign out of the hotel and head for the barn. I'll take it from here."

"Please, sir, I prefer to stay."

"Uh-uh. It's a rough game, my friend, a business for pros only. If I need you again I'll call you. They'll be checking every face that was at the reception and don't think there weren't cameras going somewhere. I don't want you picked up."

Listlessly, he said, "Very well, as you say."

I picked up the phone and asked the operator for Charlie Corbinet's number. He wasn't at the first one, but the girl told me where he could be reached and I got him at the restaurant he usually frequented, a little annoyed at having his supper interrupted until I identified myself.

"I suppose you heard, Colonel."

"Who hasn't? You're twisting a lion's tail, you know."

"Too bad. You have anything on the lab report?"

"Unofficially, yes, but I don't think it will surprise you. That needle was loaded with *condrin*. Teish would have collapsed and died of an apparent heart attack in twenty minutes all nicely blamed on the excitement of the reception and seeing himself on TV. I doubt if a doctor would have spotted it. The stuff doesn't leave a damn trace in a body for chemical analysis."

"Any source of it in the States?"

"I doubt it. The stuff's native to one area in South America. A tribe of natives use it for killing game or their enemies. It's a natural plant product and can't be synthesized chemically."

"It fits then," I told him. "Malcolm Turos' last project was centered in Brazil. He could have picked it up there."

"No doubt. Incidentally, I saw the report on the other two bodies. The guy who posed as a TV man was Parnell Rath. Two convictions for manslaughter and suspected in five homicides. He only got out of the pen three weeks ago. The one on the roof was a goofy guy he palled around with. They checked out the room Rath lived in and found a thousand bucks in small bills stashed under the window sill. Nobody's talking on this and don't you do either."

"You know me."

"Sure, that's what I'm afraid of. You pulled a cutie by locating Turos' photo. It eases some of the pressure on our relationship, but I wouldn't push too hard if I were you."

"I have no choice."

"Then a word to the wise . . . nobody, but nobody, is going to get near Teish again, that's how well they have him covered."

I laughed at him and said, "Want to bet?" and hung up while he was still firing a question at me. One of his old axioms was that the aggressor always had the advantage. I said so long to Harry, ignoring his wistful expression and went back to the elevator.

Lily Tornay's room was three floors below. I got out there, rapped on her door and identified myself when she asked who it was. This time she didn't bother hiding a gun under a towel. She couldn't have. It was all she had on. Her hair was wet and her neck and shoulders pink from the shower and she smelled deliciously soapy. "I'll wait outside if you want me to."

"Don't be funny," she snapped, not liking the grin I was giving her.

I closed the door and stepped inside. Like all dames she couldn't keep a hotel room neat to save her hide. Clothes were scattered all over the place and her Beretta was lying right in the middle of the pillow. At the foot of the bed she had a suitcase open and partially packed. "Going someplace?"

"I have orders to return. Since your latest escapade there seems little need for me to remain here."

"News travels fast."

She came over with a drink and handed it to me, the ice clinking against the glass. "My time here wasn't exactly wasted. I had an opportunity to inquire further into your background."

"And what did you find out?"

"The probable answers to several puzzling questions Interpol has fretted over. Your Martin Grady has facets to his organizations we didn't realize."

I didn't commit myself with any answer at all.

She took a sip of her drink and put it down beside her. "I do have one thing you might be interested in hearing."

"Oh?"

"We have two men in Selachin. A few hours ago they found the body of a man who was a local explosives expert. He had been shot in the head with a .38-caliber bullet of American origin. Besides Tedesco there has been another American operating in that area and he is suspected of the killing."

I still didn't say anything.

"Peter Moore, his name is," she continued. "If the dead man started the landslide that killed the technicians your country had there, he revenged them well."

"Honey," I said slowly, "did it ever occur to you that maybe the Soviets knocked him off so he couldn't talk? Thirty-eights aren't hard to come by and they'd have a lovely excuse for murder if they knew Pete was stalking them as well and looking for Tedesco."

Lily picked up the glass again, studied it, then took another small sip. "Possibly. But I think we'll know for sure before long."

My hand froze around the glass halfway to my mouth. "Why?"

She smiled enigmatically like the Mona Lisa. "Because our people have located Tedesco's hiding place and are laying a trap for the other one."

"Damn, he's alive!"

"It seems that way."

I couldn't stop the pure feeling of pleasure that went through me. My mouth stretched in a grin and I started to laugh. It took a good thirty seconds before I could stop.

"Does it seem that funny?" she asked me.

"Hell yes, sweetie. Those guys can make any trap backfire your boys try to set."

"Not when those hill people of Selachin are helping them," she added tartly.

I eased the glass down and left it there. "Honey, do you know what will happen if our men get picked up?"

"Certainly. There will be a trial and . . ."

"Nuts. They'll catch it on the spot. They'll subject them to local law and neither Interpol nor anybody else can do anything about it!"

"They put themselves in that position," she said.

Quietly, I said, "Did they?" then walked to the bed. I began to throw her stuff into the suitcase until it was filled, dumped the shells out of the Beretta so she couldn't object and snapped the bag shut.

"What are you doing?"

I reached out and stripped the towel off her with one yank and shoved her down on the bed with a scream stifled in her throat. She was all lovely and white and naked and too damn scared to even try to cover it up, her blond hair tumbling out on the covers like spilled vanilla ice cream. "You're not going anywhere for a while," I said.

"Damn you! If you think . . ."

"Remember what I told you might happen, kid?" I gave her the nastiest grin I had and she knew what I was talking about. She reached over, grabbed the spread, and flipped it on top of herself, for the first time letting a blush color her face. "Behave yourself and maybe I'll let you have your clothes back. In the meantime you stay put. I might still be able to use you."

Her voice was almost plaintive. "H-how?"

"Not like you're thinking, baby," I said.

Downstairs I checked her bag under my own name, picked up the ticket and left. Time was getting short before I called on Vey Locca and there was somebody I wanted to see first.

The big doorman greeted me with a wink and after a quick look up and down the street joined me in the lobby of the building. Rondine and my friend were still upstairs and so far he hadn't seen the man he was watching for. When I showed him Turos' photo he made an immediate identification, fixed the face in his mind and went back to the sidewalk.

I called upstairs on the house phone and told them I'd be right there, got in the automatic elevator and punched the button for Rondine's floor. Lennie Byrnes coded me through the door first before he opened it and was putting away a snubnosed .38 as I came in.

The first thing he said was, "Talbot called Miss Caine with a report. You sure have all the luck."

"I hope some of it rubs off on Tedesco and Moore. Where's Rondine?"

"Rondine? Oh . . . Miss Caine. Getting dressed."

"Any action at all?"

"Nothing."

I handed him the Turos photo to study, then put it back in my pocket. "If he knows he's identifiable by face he'll disguise himself. The only thing he can't change is his voice," I said. "You get through to Virgil Adams and see if our informants have come up with anything. We're paying ten grand for any lead and that kind of money will buy a lot of poking around." I gave him my approximate schedule, made sure he wasn't to move alone if Turos was spotted and when he went to the phone I walked over to the bedroom door and pushed it open.

She smiled at me in the mirror, a funny little smile that meant a lot of things, then swung around on the bench in front of the vanity dresser and stood up, her arms reaching out for me. The soft song of London in her voice was deep-throated and full of that wild excitement that put me on edge and with the light behind her, throwing a halo around her hair, it was like wiping out twenty years and she was her older sister, the real Rondine who had tried to kill me even while she loved me. I had to wipe the memory away fast, because even though some crazy habit made me call her Rondine too, this love was genuine and honest, full of the giving that only that kind of love could bring.

I took her in my arms and touched the wetness of her lips, felt her mouth open under mine until we satisfied each other with our nearness, then I held her off and looked at her with complete satisfaction. There was still a red welt around her throat that makeup couldn't hide and when I touched it she winced and bit her lip.

"You all right?"

"A little sore, that's all." Her eyes searched mine carefully, then: "I had a report on the reception. . . . Will you answer me something truthfully?" This time there was a careful note in her voice and I frowned at her.

"Don't push me, kid."

"I won't."

"Then ask."

"There is some speculation that the attempt on Teish El Abin's life could have been set up by your organization. Teish was impressed by your performance and has asked that you be his guest at the party being given for him by your government. Looking at it sidewise, and knowing the Grady methods, they consider this a strong possibility."

72

I dropped my hands and felt my lips pull tight across my teeth. "Three people were knocked off on that deal, sugar."

"True, and one of those killers escaped. You were there. People like that can be wasted if the results were worth it."

"You know damn well we don't operate like that!"

"I just want to hear you say it."

I nodded and tried to loosen myself up. It wasn't easy at all. "Okay, I'm saying it. I spotted the kink in that action and straightened it out. It was on the square."

She saw what had happened to me and reached for my hand. "I'm sorry, Tiger. I had to ask. It's my job too."

The tenseness seeped out of my shoulders and I let her have the smile back. "Forget it. My luck was running strong. You still supposed to stay on my tail?"

"I'd like to, but is it worth trying?"

"None of you can make it if I don't want you to."

"Then you tell me what to do."

"Are you going to that party?"

"Certainly, since you'll be invited."

"All right, but lay off me. Stick close to Vey Locca especially when she's in conversation with Teish or Sarim Shey."

"They don't talk to each other in English," she said.

"Don't worry about it. I'll take care of that."

"And what will you be doing?"

I kissed the tip of her nose and said, "Does Macy's tell Gimbel's? I'll clue you in later."

"But . . ."

"You stay on your toes. I'm going to take Lennie off you, so have one of your own people give you cover in case Turos tries for you again. Just don't be alone, got that?"

Rondine nodded seriously. She was well trained and knew the implication of what I was saying. "Very well, my Tiger." Her hand tightened around my fingers. "Do I have to be worried about you?"

"If you do, you'll be the only one. When is the party?"

"Tomorrow night at the Stacy."

"I didn't get any invitation yet."

"You will," she told me impishly. "It will probably come through Vey Locca when you see her tonight."

Softly I said, "Damn!" Then, "Who was the lip reader in that room?"

"One of our embassy people behind a panel." She made a puckish mouth at me and added, *That's* what I meant about being worried about you."

I shrugged, tilted her chin up with my hand, and said, "When things happen in the line of duty . . ."

"Duty be damned," she interrupted with a laugh. I kissed

her again and gave her a shove back toward the vanity to finish dressing and went out to Lennie.

He had completed his call to Newark and Virgil Adams had to admit a negative on Malcolm Turos. The guy had covered himself well and wasn't exposing his identity in any fashion. Men had been posted around the Russian-speaking sections of the city, the opera house and the three Broadway musicals were staked out, the specialty food houses alerted and word well spread about the price on his head. If he showed at all he was going to be nailed, but I wasn't putting too much hope on that end. That kind of net wouldn't have nailed me either. I didn't expect Turos to fall into it.

Ernie Bentley was still in his lab when I called and when I verified myself with our code he knew something was coming up. His field work was confined to the loft where he worked, but it was his world and he was an expert in it.

I said, "How small can you make a tape recorder?"

"How small do you need it?"

"Woman's compact?"

"Hell, Tiger, I have one in stock."

"Send it over to my hotel by messenger right now. Then get hold of Louis Wickhoff who does the hiring at the Stacy and arrange for him to put Lennie Byrnes on as a waiter. I want him to cover the suites Teish and Sarim Shey are using."

"Come off it, they're using regular agents on that one."

"They make sloppy waiters."

"You figure it out then."

"I'll call little Harry and have him make up some of that native slop they eat in Selachin and have him prompt Lennie on how to serve it. They have a regular ritual for that stuff and those agents won't want to expose themselves by their ignorance. One of them may go along with him into the suite, but I don't care. Have him fixed with a recorder too. Anything we pick up Harry can translate for us later, but just get Lennie in there. Louis will make him up an identity card and you fix him with the union bit. Backdate his employment for a year or so. A little loot in the right hands can kill any beefs."

"Okay, don't tell me my business."

"Just a gentle reminder. You're glued to a microscope so much I'm afraid you'll forget things."

"Yeah, picture that with you around."

I hung up, dialed Jack Brant, got him to call Harry on the phone and put the situation to him. He knew just what I wanted and knew the impression it would make, but it was going to take him awhile to get the necessary ingredients together.

74

Before I put the phone back he said, "Mr. Tiger, sir . . . I have been thinking."

"What is it, kid?"

"When I left the hotel . . . as I was getting into the elevator, I see a man knock on my door and try the knob. I do not know anybody, so why should that be? Did you send someone?"

I felt the ice again. "What did he look like?"

"Oh, nothing, I guess. Plain man in a suit."

I tried not to let him know the fear in my voice. "Probably trying the wrong room. See you later."

Lennie was watching me carefully. "What goes, Tiger?"

I turned around and picked up my hat. "Make sure somebody's with her—" I nodded toward the bedroom—"before you leave. Then check with Ernie. You know what to do?"

"I got the picture, but what's this angle?"

"When I left the Stacy I think I was followed. Damn, what a jerk I can be sometimes!"

The doorman whistled me up a cab and I climbed in, telling him to make it fast over to the Taft. He fought the traffic and earned his five bucks and I took the elevator up to Lily Tornay's room cursing the stops on the way. When I got out the door shut behind me and I ran down the corridor, around the bend and stopped in front of her door. Inside, the TV was rattling off a comedy program and I turned the knob. The door wasn't locked . . . it swung open and I went in fast with the .45 in my hand remembering every detail of where somebody could be waiting for me and ready to take a big one myself if I could blast just a single slug back.

I didn't have to. Except for Lily Tornay and the shadow people on the TV tube, the room was empty. And Lily was dead.

The nylon cording had been tied in the same fashion, but she hadn't been lucky enough to be jammed in a position that didn't allow her to move the way Rondine had. She was sprawled on the floor, hands and feet twisted up behind her back and the noose around her throat had been jerked taut by her frantic thrashings to free herself. Her nakedness was almost obscene now, her face mottled and her blond beauty gone.

Lying beside her was the note, the paperweight that held it down, her Beretta, and the message was simple. All it said was, *A Gift for a Gift, Tiger Mann.*

And it was me. I did it to her. I didn't have to be a wise guy. I could have let her clear out and she'd be alive. She passed Teddy's *Skyline* signal on to me and I let her die for it.

Well, she was going to have company. Soon.

I picked up the note, burned it and heeled the ashes into the rug. When I left I wiped the knob, walked down two flights before I picked up the elevator again and got back on the street. Deliberately, I left myself wide open for a tail, hoping Turos would make the mistake and try it. There wasn't a single device I didn't use to spot anyone following me, but after a few blocks I knew it wasn't any use. I just didn't have that feeling. If he had been there I would have known it.

Malcolm Turos was wasting his time. He had other things in mind and I would come when he was ready. On Broadway I called Charlie Corbinet and told him where to find Lily. Since she was connected with the over-all affair they'd keep it quiet until it was finished, but I was going to have some talking to do later. I could alibi myself out of it all right after the time of death was established but I didn't want any interference. Charlie said he'd go as far as he could, but not to expect any miracles.

That was enough. Time was running out fast and I was running with it. I went back to my hotel, showered and changed, told the desk clerk that any packages delivered to me were to be kept in the hotel safe and started walking across town to the Stacy.

They were waiting for me at the desk when I asked for Vey Locca, two more of the young ones with the stamp of the Washington agency on their faces. They were smiling and bright, except for their eyes, and there I could see the training they had and the mark of the orders they received. A little puzzle was there because they knew me too and couldn't figure how I fitted in at all.

My admittance was by personal invitation and they meant to see that I kept it, and that only, and were very happy to show me to Vey's room. There were more of them by every door and exit, with several carefully spotted in strategic places so that nothing went unobserved.

In the elevator they were quiet and I didn't offer them anything more than a knowing grin just to bother them a little. When we reached the door of the suite the one on my left touched the buzzer, waited until a hotel maid opened it and said, "Mr. Mann to see Miss Locca."

I watched the way the maid looked me over and knew her primary employment wasn't with the hotel. The police had this job locked. "She's waiting for him," she said. "Please come in."

I waved so long to the agency boys, handed the maid my hat and said thanks. With a look of casual disdain she tossed the porkpie on a table and led the way.

They hadn't spared any expense to make Teish El Abin's entourage comfortable. The luxury of the place rivaled a king's palace in every detail down to a private bar in the living room that matched that of any saloon in town. The maid waved her hand toward it and said, "Help yourself," with a tone no genuine maid would ever use.

Before I could mix one a cool voice from across the room said, "And you may make me one too, Tiger. Something refreshing." Vey Locca stood in the doorway smiling at me and all I could think of was that she'd never play on Broadway because she couldn't quick-change. After all this time she had finally reached the fluffy housecoat stage and that was all. She waved at the maid, a small gesture of dismissal. "You may leave now."

"But, madam . . ."

Vey Locca looked at her as if she didn't exist at all, but her voice had a hard tone of command reserved for disrespectful servants. "I said you may leave," she repeated.

This time I walked her to the door. "You do that," I told her, and when she glared at me, said, "Give my regards to the Lieutenant," and locked the door behind her.

I made a light highball for myself, a tricky bit in an old-fashioned glass for Vey, and stood swirling the ice in the glass. I heard her call out, "Bring it in here, please."

There was a full-length mirror on the wall and she stood in front of it, twisting and turning to see herself, pirouetting the way a kid would when she thinks she is alone. The brilliant white of the housecoat was a lovely contrast to the darker sheen of her skin and her hair lay like a black cloud on her shoulders. The lights on either side of the mirror silhouetted her through the sheer fabric so I could see all of her at once, a teasing vision in a deliberate pose and to make her stop I put the drink in her hand, raised my glass and said, "Lovely."

Her eyebrows arched even further, the Oriental cast to her eyes showing mock surprise. "That is all you can say?"

"Tigers don't talk much."

"Ah," she smiled, "then you *have* heard the story."

I took a pull of the highball and didn't answer her. She took a step nearer, a look of amusement crinkling the corners of her eyes.

"What do tigers do then?" she offered.

The challenge was neat and I didn't let it stand there. I grinned at her over the top of my glass and before she could move I had the neckline of that flimsy thing in my hand and tore it off her with a single wrench and it ripped with a soft sigh into a mound on the floor.

Vey Locca was one of those women who could never be called naked. She was a nude, a beautiful, provocative nude that was all high-breasted pride that swept into a gentle concave belly and serpentine thighs that swayed enticingly with an almost erotic movement. She was a tawny color, the black of her hair enriching the shade of the muted satiny texture of her skin. She seemed to ripple then, a subtle, flowing muscular movement that started at her shoulders until it came to the center of her stomach.

And in her navel she had a blood-red ruby that sparkled hypnotically, an evil eye of promise and desire that seemed to have a life of its own.

"You said I am a tiger too. I am a cat."

I never took my eyes off her. I said, "In the cat family the female doesn't give. The male takes. When he's ready."

She gave me an impertinent little smile of amusement again, stretched herself as though she were clawing for the ceiling and said, "You *are* a Tiger."

But the game was over. I was already halfway out the door headed for the bar.

I realized she had planned the whole thing when she came back before I had finished a fresh drink, a shimmering green gown molded to her body, a white mink stole hung carelessly over one arm. The only jewelry was a small diamond pendant that threw pinpoints of light from the base of her throat and her hair fell in a natural curve down onto one shoulder.

When she took the drink I made her I fingered the single diamond speculatively. "The ruby made more of an impression." I grinned into her eyes. "How do you keep it there?"

"Supposing you find out later."

"You're an engaged woman, Vey. Murders have been committed for less."

She tilted her head and agreed with a nod. "Perhaps, but there is a certain broad-mindedness adopted by cultures other than yours that do not take the same attitude."

"And yours is one?"

"Mine is one."

"Teish El Abin might think differently."

Her eyes went large a scant moment, a fiery passion there, thinking, recalling, reflecting. "I'm afraid not. Teish has certain . . . odd habits too." She finished half her drink and put the glass on the bar. "But, if you like, you may ask him yourself. We are going to join him in a few minutes."

"I thought . . ."

"It is his request. He has asked to see you. They are in his suite now waiting for us."

78

"Who are 'they'?"

"Representatives of your government."

I slid my glass over beside hers. "That ought to be interesting. Let's go." She hooked her arm under my arm and held out her hand. I turned my palm up and she dropped her key into it. "For later," she said.

There was a uniformed cop at the elevator door and two stationed beside the doors to the room. The one who admitted us was in plainclothes and the guy who stood patiently behind him was another kind of cop assigned from Washington. He recognized me with a nod and let us pass. Vey simply acted as though they were members of the hotel staff, there to serve the mighty and for nothing else.

Apparently this was a special suite, reserved for presidents and kings. The appointments were more fabulous than those in Vey Locca's apartment, the service more ornate and the quiet hush that prevailed was almost funereal. About twenty people were there, the dark blues and blacks that identified the guests sprinkled with white-coated waiters who seemed a little awkward in their ministrations, for the first time working cold because their nipped-in mess jackets didn't leave room to wear the gun that was so much a part of them.

In one corner behind a desk Teish El Abin lounged comfortably in an overstuffed armchair, a foot-long cigarette holder clamped in his teeth, the end empty. Beside him in earnest conversation with Haskell from the State Department was Sarim Shey.

I stopped to lift a drink off a tray and got a curious glance from the guy who held it while Vey went to Teish with a smile and a greeting, getting a fatherly nod in return. She kissed him affectionately, said something that brought a condescending laugh from Sarim Shey and shook hands with the dignitaries he was speaking to.

Teish said something then and Vey Locca turned, indicated me, and the old man looked past her toward me and waved his hand in greeting and with a flip of his fingers indicated that he wanted me to come over.

You could hear the change in the tone of the conversation throughout the room. The hum of it seemed to increase deliberately, and though nobody was looking, everybody was watching. Haskell's eyes were angry, and at the introduction, his handshake perfunctory. You see, we had met before. I had landed a foot in his behind one night and he never forgot it.

With the usual "Ah," Teish looked at me and said, "Mr. Mann, I would like to speak to you. Privately, of course." His small motion of the eyes was enough. The king had spoken.

Vey Locca and Sarim Shey moved off and Haskell, along with the others, excused themselves to get a drink.

Maybe the old boy was trying to feel me out. I didn't know and didn't give a good goddamn either. He was in my country and here I was king and he was just another jerkwater tourist and if he was figuring I would kiss his ass he was on the wrong horse.

I felt good enough to make it stick and said, "How're you making it, buddy?"

Teish leaned back, puzzled. "Please . . ."

"American idiom for 'How goes it?' "

He still didn't get it for a minute, then he thought it out and smiled. "Very expressive. Not . . . too understandable, but expressive."

"Watch out for us damn yankees," I said. I took a drink of the lousy martini and looked around the room. They were still watching us.

Teish said, "I have inquired into your affairs, Mr. Mann."

"Oh?"

"You have quite a sizable interest in AmPet Corporation."

Playing the executive too busy to talk to impoverished kings came easy. "One of my sidelines."

"Shall we not play games?"

I pulled a chair over and sat down next to him, wondering how much crap the other people had fed him. "Let's not," I said, not looking at him.

"AmPet Corporation originally discovered the potential of my country. It was a gallant venture, coming in there like that."

Then I threw a stopper at him. "In that case, you know you can't operate without us. We're the only ones with a process that can recover your oil."

"True. But this is not what intrigues me." He beckoned a waiter over, took a plain glass of ginger ale from the tray the guy obviously had waiting and didn't say anything until the waiter had moved off. "You are the unknown factor."

"Not if you've looked into me as you said you did."

"It's you the person I'm speaking of. For instance . . . your performance at the reception."

"My pleasure, Teish."

"Let this be my pleasure, in that case. I prefer to make . . . how do you say it?"

"First impressions."

"Ah, yes, that is it. You are aware of the situation that exists between my country and yours?"

I wanted to tell him that his country compared to this one

was like backwoods bayou, a pile of camel dung to be flushed down the sewer when you make a distinction, but for Teddy's sake and an inside straight in the poker game of international politics I let it go and let him have his illusions. All I did was nod and sip my drink, the expression I wore totally noncommittal.

Teish smiled broadly. "Then perhaps you will be interested to learn that your government and I . . . have reached an understanding. Of course there are certain remunerations to be worked out, but I prefer that the United States oversee this project. Are you pleased?"

"Up to a point," I said blandly.

"Well put, Mr. Mann." Teish grinned, amused with his bait. "I further stipulated that I prefer AmPet Corporation to handle it all."

"You won't make many friends that way," I said.

"Like you, Mr. Mann, I am not here to make friends. I gather you have many . . . shall we say, enemies? . . . here in this room, persons not satisfied with my decision. Unfortunately, they are in no position to object. Now, while we complete the arrangements, my wish is that you accompany my bride-to-be in her tour of the city and make sure she has a good time."

I put my glass down and waved off the waiter who hurried up with another. Like Teish, I waited until he was out of earshot before I said, "Wouldn't you prefer your adviser? He speaks the language. . . ."

Teish held his hand up and shook his head. "I must have him here to help me work out the details of our mutual association. Sarim is my right arm. Mr. Mann, without him I am lost. It is he who knows Western ways and the peculiarities of people outside our small country. I trust him implicitly and I must lean on him."

From the other side of the room I caught Vey Locca's eyes and she was watching us with an intense look of curiosity. I stood up and looked down at the old man in his armchair, almost surrounded by it. "I'll show her a good time, Teish."

He sat forward and leaned on the desk, his eyes sharp and bright. "Yes, you must. She is to be my bride and I intend to please her. I am the leader of many people and we must have sons. They must be the right sons that can be kings over a small but important nation. No one can influence or condemn my choice of a bride. They can only condemn me for not having sons that can lead them. Am I making myself clear, Mr. Mann?"

For the first time I saw the king of Selachin in the pathetic light that barely illuminated him. I understood his desires and his foibles, the comedy and the tragedy that went with being a king, no matter how small or large.

I said, "Loud and clear."

And all the while I felt like a stallion being put out to stud.

chapter 7

Vey Locca waited until she was in the cab before she turned her smile back on me again. She picked up the handbag that lay between us, tossed it to the other side and slid over close to me, her hand stretching out to find mine, then entwined her fingers around my own. Gently, she leaned her head over on my shoulder and thrust both legs toward the door so that the bright green hem of her dress rode up her thighs. "Do our ways seem strange to you, Tiger?"

"I've seen stranger."

"For instance," she prodded, "tell me where and when."

"And how?"

"Naturally," she said easily.

I squeezed her hand until I made her wince, grinning when I felt her stiffen beside me, but she never took her head away. "The world is all alike, baby. There's nothing you can't find in it that you can't find right here in New York. It's Alpha and Omega, the beginning and the end. The dirty and the beautiful, the lusty and the frigid. There's life and death in your own back yard and sex with all its variations. You only see what you want to see and whatever you look for you'll find. What do you want to see?"

"The tiger."

"They don't walk out on a lawn to be fawned over like housecats, sugar. They stay in the jungle and grow and live because nobody's been able to kill them. They're nightwalkers with an incredible intuition and finely trained senses that allow them to survive. If you want a tiger you have to go looking for one and even then you have to be careful because the chances are he'll find you first and then you're dead."

"But when a tiger finds another tiger looking for him . . . ?"

I let go her hand and tapped the driver on the shoulder. "Stop at the next corner."

Vey said, "You didn't answer me."

"Maybe he'll take her head off. Maybe he'll nudge her back to his hidy-hole and eat her alive."

"Take me back to your hidy-hole, Tiger," she asked me.

I looked sidewise into those great black eyes and said, "Drop dead," and she grinned back and stuck out her tongue.

She didn't like the first place I took her for a drink. It was all tourists wearing trophies from the World's Fair in their pockets, too loud and commercial, and even though it was a segment of New York she wanted to leave. We tried the bistros where price came before quality and the slop chutes where the bums had to be brushed off like flies and the queer joints from lower Broadway to the upper Fifties, yet nothing seemed to satisfy her.

Before it closed we dropped into the Blue Ribbon on Fortyfourth for something real in gourmet eating and with Augie presiding she indulged herself in an outlandish plate of a German specialty while I put a sizzling platter of Welsh Rabbit away. Only then did she do what every woman does, sit back and say, "That's what I wanted."

Beside us, Augie smiled and lit her cigarette for her. He's a funny guy with a weird sensitivity. He never inquired about her origin nor was he told, but he knew. He sensed other things about her I was reluctant to admit, but he was in a position to force the issue just to make me uncomfortable. "Perhaps the lady would like to see . . . well, some of her homeland." He looked down at her, still smiling. "Is that so?"

"You are very astute, Augie. What do you suggest?"

Then he dropped it in my lap. He shrugged and indicated me. "Ask Tiger. He knows. If it is in the city, he can take you there."

Vey Locca smiled at me, the edges of her teeth a glaring white against the dark maroon of her mouth. She tucked her lower lip between them a moment and cocked her head inquisitively. "You were supposed to entertain me, you know."

Augie knew when to duck out. He said good night to us both and retired somewhere out of sight and I said, "Say it then. What do you want to see?"

Vey sucked deeply on the cigarette, then let the smoke out in a thin, hazy cloud through pursed lips. "Do I really have to tell you?" she asked.

"No." I reached for her stole and held it out for her to shoulder into. "With modifications. There are still laws in this state. I could go all the way but I don't want to play guns with a broad hanging on my arm."

We grabbed a cab on the corner of Broadway and I told him to take us downtown to the Turkish Gardens. The driver looked back, grinned and nodded, then took off into traffic, threading his way through the other cabs around Times Square. He cut over and took Ninth Avenue down past the darkened faces of the office buildings, staying with the lights until we were in another part of the city that so few knew about.

The Turkish Gardens were on the second floor of an old building with twisting stairs leading up that sagged and creaked underfoot. Halfway up you began to hear the sensual tinkling of bells and the rhythmic beat of drums that throbbed through the thin walls. Neither the instruments nor the music were native to New York. They had come off the streets of Istanbul, transported here by a farseeing immigrant who knew the tastes of his own kind would never leave them.

I opened the door and let Vey walk into the haze of blue smoke that rose from the multitude of cigarettes and cigars to boil at the ceiling before being sucked into the maw of two exhaust vents on either side of the room.

The one who let us in bowed, spoke a greeting in a terse tongue and led us to a table. I could feel the excitement going through Vey, saw it in the set of her shoulders and the sway of her hips. Her head bobbed to and fro with the tempo until she sat down and when I saw her face there was a wild exhilaration there.

As lovely as she was, as many as were there, nobody turned to look at her. Every eye was riveted on the dancer that snaked her way across the floor, the last piece of her costume clutched in her hand like a token of victory. She was a big girl, lusty, heavyset, glistening with sweat that made her skin shine as she made every muscle in her body tremble to the increasing pace of the music. There were bells on her fingers and toes accentuating every studied movement, their tinkling almost too rapid to believe.

Little by little the music reached a feverish pitch before it touched a climax of madness and left the dancer on her knees, body arched and her head nearly touching the ground while she performed the final ritual with no movement except the undulation of her stomach.

The audience was explosively silent a moment, a hushed gasp of approval before they were back to reality. But they hardly had time to clap their appreciation before someone moved at a table and another woman was on the floor.

This one was no professional, but as much a part of the

performance as the other. She had been caught up in the wildness of the moment and it was coming out of her as she took the heat of the drum and began to writhe with some hidden ingenuity that belonged only to the few that had a complete understanding of the passion that flowed from the musicians behind her.

Twice, she circled the small dance area before she made a languid move toward the buttons at the back of her dress. One by one she flipped them open, snaked herself out of the encumbrance, and stood there briefly, arms outstretched, her entire body a blur of motion. At the tables each pair of eyes took in every movement, nodding appreciatively at each new variation, waiting patiently for another development, and when she loosened her brassiere and let it fall there was a murmur of satisfaction.

Nothing was disappointing about this one. She was full-blossomed, with breasts that were firm, individual things of beauty that gyrated in a dance all their own, flaring hips that twitched and jerked, and willowy legs that bent slowly until the floor was her bed and she was in the throes of some grandiose dream.

Each second the music grew until her movements became spasmodic and a silent scream formed her mouth, eyes wide and glassy. Someone at the tables began throwing bills and others followed, bills of all denominations, some fluttering to drift lazily across her bare stomach, some to float carelessly to the floor. And once again the music ended in a wild, pulsating clash of brass and flutes with the drum a mad overtone behind it.

Nobody clapped. It was as if they were drained of emotion. They sat there while the dancer left the floor and another woman picked up the pieces of her clothing to take to her. I must have ordered drinks unconsciously because a waiter set down two on our table and picked up the bill I left there. Just as unconsciously Vey took hers, sipped from it as the band started again, then suddenly spilled it down her throat as if she were parched.

Something had happened to her eyes. They were narrow slitted, the cant of them more pronounced. Her lips seemed fuller as if she had them between her teeth, and her breasts rose and fell deeply with each slow breath she took. A faraway flute came in then, the eerie sound of it muffled at first before becoming more pronounced. There were more bells, a cymbal, and some strange woodwind that called until it was heard. The lights changed, dimming to a pale blue, and those at the tables around the floor waited expectantly, knowing that it would happen, not impatient, just waiting.

The flute called again and Vey Locca rose from her chair.

I didn't try to stop her.

Hers was not a dance like the others. There was a blending of the cultures in this one, a new factor that was sensed at once. The mark of the Orient was there all right, the wild purity of each studied action belonged to a world far away, but it was the *blending* of the tribal rituals that made it so different.

She stood in the middle of the floor, eyes closed, her mouth glossy wet and partly open, never seeming to move her feet, yet slowly going through a classic series of postures, each one designed to put the fire of the music, the heat of the dance inside you. Somehow the dress slipped down her shoulders, then with a shrug she dropped it and her breasts were bared, orange-tipped against nearly purple skin in the blue light.

Under my feet I could feel the floor tremble as the audience tapped out the rhythm, bodies moving as Vey exposed each new delight to their rapt gaze. Slowly the dress fell further, then dropped down her hips as her torso bowed backward and her hair tumbled until it touched the floor.

In her navel the blood-red ruby looked bloodier than ever as it winked its evil eye at the hundreds of eyes watching and as she turned I had the feeling that it was watching me alone.

It was too intense a moment to prolong. It had to end and it stopped on a death note of the flute that drifted back into the shadow where it had emerged from. She didn't walk away. She stood there long enough to slip her arms back into the dress and go through the conjurer's motion that clothed her in a single instant. Only then did she walk out of the lights back to the table to the silent applause of the crowd that watched her.

When she sat down her breath came fast, but not from the activity on the floor. There was more there and it showed in her eyes. She took the other drink I had ordered, swallowed thirstily without tasting it, and only then did she see me across the table and smile like a woman who has just been made love to.

"You were great," I said.

Her tongue passed over her lips and she ran her fingers through her hair to make it swirl across her shoulder again. "It has been a long time," she mused. "There are many things . . . I have missed. You were truly pleased?"

"Truly."

"I can . . . do better."

"I don't see how."

"But you will, my Tiger, I will dance alone for you one time. Soon."

The men on the bandstand left their places and others took

over. There was still a foreign flavor in their renditions, but not the frantic passion there was before. Someone started singing, others joined in, then the calls for drinks had the waiters scurrying during the musical intermission.

It was a stout bald-headed man who made me turn around. He shouted something in Greek, stood up and began to clap madly while the rest at his table took up the cheers. I had to lean out to see around them and spotted the loner at a tiny corner table hidden in the darkness. Whoever he was, he had the approval of one bunch anyway.

The one handling the baby spots swung the fresh pink light his way and cut through the shadows and I could see him plainly, a sharp-featured guy under a shock of thick black hair with a drooping mustache dressed in a beat-up brown corduroy coat and turtle-necked sweater.

For once the Greek turned to English as they started to shout, "Sing! Sing! The Bocallo . . . sing!" clapping madly to make the guy turn on his voice. He waved them off with a faint smile, trying to get out of the lights, but they were too insistent. The stout Greek left his table, half ran to the corner and tried to pull the man to his feet, then turned around and yelled to his friends, "It is he! Paris, Madrid, Moscow . . ." The rest was lost in Greek, but the occasional words they spoke made it plain enough that they had a famous baritone among them.

And this one wouldn't sing.

He couldn't. He had a hole in his throat.

I tore the .45 from my belt and cocked it as I shoved my way through the packed crowd that surrounded him. Under their eager hands the turtle neck of the sweater came down and I could see the scar just as he saw me. In wild desperation he burst through those nearest to him, cut across the dance floor while I fought to get a clear shot at his back.

There were too many people there, too many wondering what was happening and pushing in for a closer look. He was swallowed in a group by the door before I got there and when I reached him it was hissing shut slowly on its pneumatic dampener. It took a look at the rod to get them out of the way and I scrambled down the stairs to the street, taking the steps three at a time.

My luck wasn't with me this time. The red taillights of a taxi were disappearing down the broad expanse of the avenue and there wasn't another one in sight.

Malcolm Turos had stepped out for an evening of his favorite entertainment and almost stepped into his own grave. But I knew one thing now. He wasn't that smart after all. There was a nick in his professional technique and that chink in the armor was going to kill him. I stopped, and put the gun away and thought about it. Someplace he had already exposed himself.

I had the manger tell Vey I was waiting for her outside. He was glad to do it. He didn't understand what had happened and didn't ask for an explanation. All he wanted was for me to be out, although he watched Vey Locca go reluctantly. I took her hand and led her down the stairs, went to the corner and whistled a cab over.

Once we were inside she said, "You will tell me now why you did what you did?"

I let the anger that was seething inside me ease out. If the Turkish Gardens hadn't been my own choice I would have spelled it out *trap* and Vey Locca would be somewhere in a soundproofed room talking her head off to beat the pain of what I'd do to her. But it *had* been my choice. Coincidence was not the factor. It was the same set of primary impulses working toward a common end. Two people from another continent sought a mutual pleasure and chance dropped it into my lap.

"That man was Malcolm Turos," I said.

Vey Locca was lighting a cigarette, holding the tip of the flame from a gold Ronson to the end of the holder. When I mentioned his name it never flickered; there was no involuntary start of fear or surprise on her part at all, and she was either a great actress or a cool woman under pressure. "He's the one who tried to kill Teish," I added.

The lighter jumped then. She snapped it shut, inhaled and looked at me sharply. "You . . . knew he'd be there?"

"No."

"Then how . . . ?"

"He's in a strange country. He has time. He's waiting. He won't frequent the usual places you might expect him to, but boredom finally caught up with him and he went for one of his oddball kicks. The Gardens feature things that are native to Europeans, are off the general tourist trail with something to his liking. He never expected to be recognized there, even in a wig and mustache, but that sharp-eyed Greek spotted him and remembered when he was an outstanding singer overseas. That, baby, was pure luck that I blew. Damn it, I could have had him cold if I could have gotten through the mob. One shot would have brought him down and I couldn't make it."

When she was quiet for a long minute I knew I had said too much. Without looking at me Vey asked, "Who are you really, Tiger?"

Right then I jumped back into my act again. "Sugar, in this business of high finance you don't slouch around in an office.

You work the fields and the city streets. I've been in as many revolutions as I have legal conferences and too many times you stay alive because you're first with a gun out and ready to gamble. AmPet has located and developed sixteen new oil fields in seven countries within the last seven years and done reclamation work previously thought impossible. We have processes that are years ahead of everybody else's and to stay ahead we have to fight everything from governments to gunmen to stake a claim or hold it. To be an executive with us means you have to know every phase of the operation and if ever the theory of the survival of the fittest was proven, it's in our racket.

"I'm just the guy you see, honey, no more, no less. Maybe I sneaked in the back door, but I'm here and here I stay. I don't think anybody is fooling anybody any longer. There's a pressure play going on and a lot of people are in on the bite. When you're dealing in power or money you're dealing in death and anyone near the scene is a target. I just happened to be better equipped than most."

Vey's hand ran down the side of my leg and she smiled, the Manchurian slant of her eyes like arrows in the semidarkness. "Tiger," she said, "I don't think I believe you."

"And I don't give a damn, either."

"*That* I believe." She squeezed my leg, then patted it.

"Tell me about you," I said abruptly.

Amused, she let out a little chuckle. "The truth, or would you like a wonderful lie? I think I prefer to tell you a beautiful story about me because I enjoy that best."

"Suit yourself. If I wanted to know about you I'd make one phone call and twenty-four hours later I'd have every detail of your life from the day you were born."

"Then perhaps I should save you the trouble." She tapped the ashes from her cigarette to the floor. "My mother was half Chinese, half Russian, my father was Irish-Japanese, and if you can find a more quaint amalgamation of the races, I can't picture it. Would you like the sordid details of my early life?"

"Not especially. When did you meet Teish?"

"Three years ago. I was in Morocco. He was looking for a wife and his agents saw me dance. There is more to it than that, but that is sordid too. I agreed to his terms and they took me to Selachin. Let us say I was satisfied with the prospect and stayed."

"He had a wife then."

"I was employed as his secretary until she died."

"Well planned," I said.

"They too took their chances. As I said, there are customs still in existence that seem abhorrent to . . . foreigners. No outside influence will ever change them so they must be accepted. In spite of all the religious indoctrination of the Western world the Haitians still practice voodooism. In places there is still human sacrifice, slave trade and head-hunters. Are we so different?"

The cab pulled to the curb in front of the Stacy before I could answer her. I got out, paid him off and took her arm up the steps. The two men apparently engaged in casual conversation stationed there watched us, then followed us until we were on the elevator. Another stepped in with us but didn't get off at our floor. He didn't have to. Hal Randolph was sitting in a straight back chair talking to Dick Gallagher and making a great play of totally ignoring us.

I took the key she had given me earlier, opened her door and let her pass inside. A new maid was there this time, a tall heavy-set woman with tight iron-gray hair and an expression that comes from working the tough end of town where the sweet-girl type could suddenly jump you with a knife and emaciated punks edgy for a blast of H in their veins could erupt into pure hell when they thought they were going to be cut off.

Vey said, "That will be all. You may leave now."

Like the other one, she was reluctant to go, but had no choice. I went through the same routine, making sure she was out, then bolting the door. If Malcolm Turos got through the police screen they had set up he had to be a genius.

It didn't take long to locate the four bugs planted in the suite. There didn't seem to be too much effort expended in hiding them so I assumed they were there to be found and the occupants to have a false sense of security. With the electronic advances, voice pickup, even remote, was no problem and any decent expert could rig a mike hookup that couldn't be detected. Just to be lousy I snapped the heads off the button mikes I found and dropped them in an ash tray. Vey Locca watched, a humorous smile on her mouth, apparently not unfamiliar with this sort of thing.

Kings and their cohorts always had their problems.

She walked to the walnut hi-fi set against the wall, chose a few records and placed them on the changer. "This way is even better to eliminate eavesdropping."

I could have told her she was wrong, but I didn't. Frankly, I didn't care.

It was night music that came from the speaker, soft, mellow tones I had never heard before. Night music from another world, and when I stretched out on the couch and closed my eyes I could visualize fog and empty marketplaces, a stealthy figure crossing a rooftop, and the glint of moonlight on the downward thrust of a knife. It was sensual, picturesque . . . you couldn't listen without seeing the images it invoked.

I knew when Vey Locca was in the room because she was part of the image and I could feel her presence. While my eyes were closed she had dimmed the lights so that only one small lamp threw a dull yellow light through the star-shaped perforations in its shade, casting weird patterns on the wall and ceiling.

When I turned my head I saw her, not as she was at the Turkish Gardens, not performing a blending of rituals, but nude, deliciously nude, a wild, wanton, pagan nude, not oblivious to the presence of another in the room, but completely conscious of the fact, directing every essence of her nudity toward that one in a tantalizing manner as if an impenetrable wall of glass separated them so that she could taunt and torture with immunity, laying a feast of desire before a starving man who could see and smell and want, but couldn't get through the barrier.

Her eyes were bright, moving like darts, watching to enjoy the torment she was stirring up; her lips were wet, parted to show the gleaming white of her teeth. She was wide-shouldered and with supple breasts that were swelled with passion, impertinent in their pride of freedom, her sucked-in stomach softly ridged with muscles that played like little fingers under her skin, then ran vertically down her thighs and calves until she became an artist's study in anatomy.

And all that while the blood-red ruby in her navel was a focal point that kept calling and she waited for me to move.

She came closer to the invisible wall, tempting me with her delights, daring me, and when she couldn't fathom my response became even more abandoned in her offering.

It was she who broke the barrier down. She had laid the feast but had given way to her own hunger and knew that the prisoner was really herself and threw herself across the space that separated us with a moan torn from her own throat, then she was a warm, slithering thing that tried to smother me with a passion she could no longer suppress.

The image was gone, the reality was there. The nudity was gone too . . . she was naked now, perfumed and slippery, searching, demanding, insisting upon the absolute fulfillment.

The blood-red ruby was in my hand and I didn't remember taking it from her.

Hal Randolph had waited patiently for me. He could afford to. I could have avoided him by going down the stairwell but then there would have been another time and there was no point in avoiding him. When he saw me he pressed the buzzer for the elevator and we stood there together until it arrived, then rode down silently together.

The lobby was almost deserted at that hour and those who were there were too alert to be guests and if you looked closely you could see the rise under their coats where the guns were slung. We walked out to the steps and watched the city in the only hours that it ever dozed and Randolph said, "You were supposed to stop in for a talk."

"I intended to."

He pulled a pack of butts from his pocket, shook one out and lit it. "We checked you out in that AmPet deal. Grady might have made a bad deal there." His eyes took me in carefully to catch my reaction.

"I doubt it. His lawyers are as good as your tax men."

"Maybe." He shrugged unconcernedly. "There's another problem. Lily Tornay. It took long enough for the story to get to us and some people are getting mad. We have the report on Edith Caine too."

"Don't squeeze me, Hal. I can verify every minute of my time if I have to and I don't want to get tied up."

"You may have to."

"Do I?"

He flipped the unsmoked cigarette away in anger and it went out in a shower of sparks on the sidewalk. "Damn you, Tiger, it's gone too far. We have to give in to the demands of that creep Teish because State wants it that way, but I don't have to take too much crap from you."

"Drop it, Randolph. You know who you want. Every department in the country has a flyer out on Malcolm Turos, not me. I almost had him for you earlier and he broke loose, but . . ."

"What!"

I gave it to him the way it had happened, enjoying the red that seemed to explode into his face. When I finished I said, "But don't lay it on me, buddy. I'm a private citizen and not subject to departmental orders and there is no warrant out for my arrest. You can try anything you like, but you damn well know I'll blow the whistle to the papers and this whole deal will turn into a propaganda piece for the Reds. If you don't think I'll save my skin any way I have to or shove something up your tail just to be lousy, then you don't know me any more."

Randolph's mouth tightened and he took out another cigarette and stuck it in his mouth without lighting it. He thought a moment, then twisted his lips in a nasty grin. "You made one mistake, Tiger. You asked for it and you got it." He reached in his breast pocket and found an envelope, tapped it against his palm a moment and handed it to me. "Yours under protest. Temporary assignment to a section of the Army Intelligence. You *do* come under orders now. Sign two copies and keep one for youself." He handed me a pen. "You're cleared to carry that rod, but keep in mind the penalties that go with your active status now, and all I want to do is catch you in an infraction of the rules and you've had it."

I laughed at him, signed the copies, and handed them and the pen back. "I'll have to tell Teish thanks. He knows how to put the pressure on."

Randolph ignored the sarcasm, his voice cold. "We'll want a report on your intentions and your actions. You are to make no attempt to do more than you're told to. Tomorrow night you'll be at that goddamn party with the rest of us in a protective capacity only. I.A.T.S. has the full picture of Grady's AmPet operation but you aren't working for him now. I'm hoping either one of you make the move that gives us a chance to slam you."

"The boys in Washington have tried long enough," I reminded him. "But how the hell are ten-thousand-a-year clerk types going to buck the brains of a guy who can make thirty million a year? That's the trouble with this country . . . some damn petty politician or pseudo-statesman or senator who talked his way from sharecropping to D.C. thinks he can cross minds with the people who really made this country great. They hate because they're jealous and try to stop the only ones who can keep us on top. They organize their tiny minds and legislate control of business and industries they couldn't get a job in as janitors and the population squirms under their heels. Brother . . . you have a case. The big ones are getting tired. They're doing something about it. They're going to make sure we win despite all the damn stupidity and fear you find in the mice."

"But not you," Randolph said. "You won't have a thing to do with it."

"Try me and see," I said. I shoved my copy of the orders in my pocket and went on down the steps. Behind me I heard Randolph let out a laugh and didn't like it. He should have been fuming, but he wasn't.

From the hotel I called Newark Control and told them what had happened at the Gardens. Virgil Adams questioned me in detail, his voice sleepy, got it down on the tape for transcription later, then said, "Johnson called from London. Interpol's all het up about the Lily Tornay thing and another agent's on the way over."

"It'll keep. She told me Tedesco's alive. What's that bit?"

"Correct. Pete Moore made a contact and they're both holing up somewhere in the hills. Pete took a short-wave transmitter in with him . . . limited power so he only had time for one broadcast and that was terse."

"Some local dynamite expert was knocked off. He do it?"

"Negative. That was a Soviet action. They have a team in there and are using that as an excuse to hunt down Pete and Teddy. Interpol was involved but got out in a hurry when they saw what was developing. Pete's staying with Teddy . . . he was hit in the thigh and can't get around."

"How does it look?"

"Rough."

"Can they make it?"

"Pete signaled R-1 which means they haven't a chance the way things are. All borders are clamped down and nobody wants to touch the situation. It's a real powder keg, Tiger."

"Somebody has to go in after them."

"Impossible and not authorized. We can't afford it. The only one who can change things is Teish. One word from him can stop everything."

"Okay, Virg, you'll get the word."

"When? Those guys can't hang on much longer. It's a real scramble. If it were a city they'd have a chance, but not in hills they're unfamiliar with and with those damn natives like bloodhounds."

"Tomorrow night. I'll get it for you."

"I hope so."

I hung up, pounding my fist into my palm. One way or another, I had to squeeze Teish. Each push had to be calculated because if it went wrong he could lean in the opposite direction. He was out after his own ends and meant to get them. He had what everybody wanted and if he thought one side was trying to take it from him he'd jump to the other for his own protection.

As late as it was I called Ernie Bentley at his home and got him out of the sack. He yawned and said, "Don't you ever sleep, Tiger?"

"When it's necessary. Did you get Lennie Byrnes set?"

"He's in. It cost, but he'll be ready. He's been double-checking back with your girl but everything's tight. Talbot was called off on another deal and left a woman with her who's an agent for their embassy. Lennie didn't want to take any chances so he got Frankie Hill to stay on the street outside. Those dupe shots of Turos help any?"

"They got me a little edge and off the hook a bit. The guy isn't going clean like the pictures show."

"Didn't think he would. After you left I made up some more and retouched them with assorted hair and facial disguises. You want to pick them up?"

"Let's expedite matters. Have a runner drop them off with Charlie Corbinet. He'll know what to do with them. Get to it the first thing."

"Done. Need anything?"

"Just sleep. I'll check with you tomorrow."

I put the phone back and started getting ready for bed. I checked my coat pockets before I took it off. In the right-hand one was the blood-red ruby and I put it on the night table. I still didn't see how she had kept it in her navel.

chapter 8

I awoke with the rain beating against the window, coming in the gap at the sill in a fine spray. It was noon, but the sky was a dirty gray that roiled at the tops of the buildings, swallowing their upper levels, seeming to dissolve them before they were even digested.

For a few minutes I lay there, trying to recapture the thought that brought me into wakefulness. It had come out of the recesses of my memory, tapped me lightly demanding recognition, then fled before I could lay hands on it and lay back there out of sight like a dark blob. In front of it was the face of Malcolm Turos grinning at me. No, it wasn't a grin, it was a silent laugh of derision.

Sometimes it happens that way. I knew that elusive thought was the end of a thread that could lead to him. Someplace it was offered to me and I had rejected it. It had come and gone in an instant, captured by an involuntary sensory process, but lost in the unconscious mind that emerged only when there was no control.

I rolled out of bed, shaved and dressed, then went downstairs for coffee. When I finished I climbed in a phone booth and called Dick Gallagher. Earlier he had gotten copies of Ernie Bentley's retouched photos of Turos and had them distributed, but as yet there was no news.

Charlie Corbinet didn't have anything else to add except warn me that something new was in the wind concerning the Senate committee's investigation of Martin Grady. He couldn't put a finger on it, but the word was spreading that the committee had an angle to work on now. I wasn't worried about Grady protecting himself so I thanked him and hung up.

I went back to the desk and picked up the compact Ernie had sent over, signed out for it and examined the miniature recorder enclosed under the thin mirror. Lennie would have one like it on him when he was in the hotel and might be able to pick up something useful. It was an outside chance, but you had to cover all bets.

At a newsstand I picked up a morning edition of the paper and scanned through it. The front page had a shot of the body on the sidewalk outside the Stacy, listing the person as a suicide, an out-of-work man despondent and sick who somehow got to the roof undetected and stayed there until he had worked up nerve enough to jump. He had narrowly missed hitting several people walking below.

The other man was reported to be an accidental death that occurred while he was fixing a television set. The explanation was brief and sufficiently vague to invite little curiosity. Although his name was given, there was no mention of his prior prison record. I.A.T.S. had done a beautiful cover-up and it was unlikely that any more would be said. Even the guests in the room when the attempt was made on Teish's life were unaware of what had happened. It was too fast and their attention was centered somewhere else. Being hustled from the room was only natural under the circumstances and the less said the better. That type was inclined to say only what they were told to say and weren't offering anything for free.

Although I went over every item in the paper from front to back, there was not even a squib about Lily Tornay. She lived and died anonymously, her death buried in the police files, and if the case were never closed there still would be nothing written about her except in a letter to her family if she had one.

It was the nature of the business. Like the Air Corps song, you live in fame and go down in flame. Nobody saw you go. There was nothing left to see anyway.

I pulled the collar of my trench coat up around my ears while the rain dripped down off the brim of my hat. The taxis were filled going by, the drivers happy with the unending business, never having to cruise for a fare, faces blankly ignoring those who didn't make it in time as they discharged passengers, friendly only to those already inside.

Except for the few equipped with raincoats or umbrellas hugging the sides of the buildings to stay out of the driving wet, I had the sidewalk to myself. I turned west and started walking toward the U.N. building complex whose main structure still rose like a giant air conditioner over the side of the city, not caring whether I got drenched or not.

My mind kept reaching for that evasive little piece of information that danced around back there like an invisible dervish trying to make itself heard, and when it did, scampered away and hid again. By the time I reached the U.N. I gave up the mental chase and located a page I knew to go collect Miss Caine. He said she was at a special session and I'd have to wait so I walked around the pile of masonry dedicated to peace, listening to the war talk and mingling with the tourists who thought it was all part of the World's Fair.

Rondine took twenty minutes before she broke loose and I followed her into the lounge that we had to ourselves for a change. I didn't feel loose with her this time. I kept remembering the blood-red ruby and meeting her eyes wasn't easy. If she had any intuitive feeling about it at all it didn't show or else she understood, because she was there in my arms, ready for the way I held her and I knew that nothing was ever going to tear this woman from me.

"I only have a few minutes, Tiger."

"Sure." I handed her the compact and told her what I had in mind. She was to keep it with her at the party that night and cover Vey Locca if she digressed from a language she couldn't understand. I said, "How close is your embassy working on this?"

"Tight. They met this morning with your people and have everything arranged. Did you know that Teish has asked specifically for AmPet?"

I nodded.

"You might be interested in something else."

"Like what?"

"This is restricted information, but since you'll find out about it anyway I'll tell you now. There was another meeting this morning and one of our staff was invited in an advisory capacity. Teish is going to ask for a . . . a . . . how do you call it?"

"Handout?"

Rondine grinned at me. "Crazy Americans. Really, it's a long-term loan and a sizeable sum. He had already made overtures in London and it's still under consideration, but I think your government will come through with it. Of course, it's still unofficial and has to go through the usual channels, but it can't afford to be ignored."

"He's working fast," I said.

"Teish has to."

"I suppose he guarantees repayment if the oil recovery is successful."

"Exactly. And from what I gather, AmPet is the only company far enough advanced in their research to handle it."

I let out a short laugh. "I can see them putting the heat on Martin Grady now. He's holding all the hole cards and if the

99

deal goes through he'll be bigger than ever with a club over their heads they won't forget."

"Perhaps."

The way she said it made me lose the smile. Behind her words there was a depth of meaning and I said, "What's the angle?"

"Do you know Seaton Coleman and Porter Lockwood?"

Mention either one of them and my back would crawl. "Damn right I do. They're giveaway artists who kick over American business to those lousy little dictators who stamp their feet and wave their fists. Those slobs push their screwball idealist notions into our diplomacy and figure billions lost to our economy is worth some country's going to the democratic scheme of things when it's really a Commie power play. Where do they come into it?"

"I shouldn't eavesdrop, but I was in a position where I couldn't help but hear. They have a clique ready to start action that will take AmPet right out of Martin Grady's hands and put it under government control. They have enough influence to do it, or at least enough to cause trouble. I wouldn't even tell you this, but I have certain ideals too and this pair were responsible for some of the difficulties our government encountered when they were trying to retain control of some parts of the Empire."

"Okay, doll, thanks for the word. If Grady moves fast enough he can forestall any action. Those damn stripedpantsers aren't going to louse this job up. Not if I can help it." I kissed the tip of her nose and she crinkled it at me. There would have been more, but the door opened behind me to admit a half dozen men all talking at once. "See you tonight. Make sure you aren't alone."

"Talbot's with me. He's picking me up at eight. Everybody is so jumpy they travel in threes and fours."

"I'm not worried about the others. Turos is picking his target and he'll wait for the right time. He's not fanatic enough to lose his own hide when he doesn't have to so I'm not worried about him trying for a hit out in the open. Whatever he does will be well thought out with an escape route ready for himself. He's a pro with a hell of a lot of experience. He'll make his move knowing what our countermeasures are. What we have to do is hope he slips somewhere along the line."

Rondine lifted herself on her toes and kissed me lightly on the mouth. "Please, Tiger . . . be careful."

"You know me, kid."

"That's the trouble," she said, "I do."

On the way back I leaned against the wind and the rain until

100

I reached the Stacy. My friend was at his desk in the personnel office when I stuck my head in and he nodded an okay and made a motion with his finger to come in. At my request he phoned back to have Harry come in, ostensibly to make sure he had everything needed to prepare the specialties the house was serving to Teish.

Little Harry was all smiles, his face wreathed in pleasure, and when I had him alone he told me that there had been no trouble at all setting the plant up. He had coached Lennie in the proper procedure, secured all the necessities and been assigned a place in the kitchen to cook them, out of sight of the chef who thought the whole mess was too disgusting even to look at. Lennie had made several trips to the suite, always accompanied by another waiter, and had made numerous contacts with Teish and Sarim Shey who seemed pleased by the unexpected service.

Vey Locca had been there twice, but had not been asked to stay for any of the discussions. Evidently she operated on a social level for Teish, but at various times had been in conversations with several of the dignitaries who seemed impressed by her political awareness and ability to influence Teish's decisions.

When he gave me the picture I let him go back to work, made an okay sign to my friend and went out to the lobby. I called Vey on the phone, knowing it was bugged. The screening didn't take long. I was a cog in the machine now, unwanted, but necessary for a side phase of the operation.

Vey came on with a throaty hello and said, "You have waited a long time to call me, Tiger."

"You knew I would."

"Certainly. But I have waited. I find it hard to forget you."

"I have something to return to you."

Her laugh was warm and low. "Yes, I know. Tonight. You will call for me."

"I thought you would be escorted by Teish."

"He will be in conference until the last minute. I believe they have you under discussion. Tomorrow you will be invited to attend a rather important meeting."

"I'd rather hear about tonight."

"At eight I shall be ready. Not in a robe."

"I prefer the robe."

"So do I, but unfortunately it cannot be. Another time, another place and there will be many more things. Once a queen and there will be little left for me."

"Except," I said.

"Yes," she repeated, "except. I wonder how long the enjoyment of them will last. I'm afraid I will always be thinking of the jungle and the tiger I gave up for them."

I didn't answer her.

"Tonight at eight," she told me and I heard the phone click dead.

I started to move away from the partitioned row of phones when a porter went by pushing a floor polisher toward the service door at the end of the short hallway. He opened it with a key, reached back for the polisher, when I saw the figure go past in the opening, taking the steps two at a time. I only had a glimpse, but the face was that of Sarim Shey.

Before I could grab it, the door closed shut behind the porter and with the noise the polisher was making on creaky wheels I knew he'd never hear the pounding of my fist against the steel. I ran back to the desk, waved the clerk over and pointed to the door. "Where does that lead to?"

"Why?"

"I thought I saw a friend of mine coming down."

He shook his head. "I doubt it. That's just a service stairwell that leads to the back alley. It's not a fire exit."

"What's the quickest way there?"

"You'll have to go around the building from the east side. There's an alley that goes up there, but I'm sure you're making a mistake. I can tell . . ."

But I didn't wait to hear the rest of the sentence. I got back outside, cut up the street, turned the corner of the building and trotted against the rain until I found the alley. A grilled gate was open there and a taxi was pulling off, already halfway down the street, but hugging the left side as though it had been parked there.

In the alley, lounging against the wall under the overhang above the service entrance was Sarim Shey puffing slowly on a long black cigar. He never bothered to look at me, but blew a stream of smoke out to dissipate in the rain with a satisfied expression on his face.

Whatever Sarim Shey had come down to do was already done.

I didn't think it was to find solitude to smoke a cigar.

Before he could notice me I walked on past, crossed the street to the newstand on the opposite corner and went inside where the fat guy behind the counter was staring disconsolately out into the gray afternoon. "Was there a taxi across the street a minute ago?"

I got the blank New York stare when you ask leading questions. I tried to find an annoyed look and said, "Damn, I told her to wait. . . ." and let it drift off there.

And like all New Yorkers who enjoy being a part of other

people's problems, but who can't get hurt by them, he said, "Oh . . . yeah, I seen one."

"Stand there long?"

His shoulders hunched in a shrug. "Didn't notice. Just seen one, thassal. What happened?"

"Broads," I said disgustedly.

The guy agreed with me. "Yeah, them."

I walked back on the opposite side of the street from the hotel and looked down the alley. Sarim Shey was gone, but most of his cigar was still lying there smoking on the concrete. Upstairs somebody was going to catch hell for leaving him alone that long, but that was their trouble. Just the same, I wondered how he managed it.

I had a coded note waiting for me at the hotel to call Virgil Adams. When I rang him he said, "Stay put, Tiger. I have a man coming up in a few minutes. Remember Casey Ballanca?"

"We worked together ten years ago."

"He's got the poop. More information on Turos. Stay in close contact with us if you can."

"Don't worry, I will."

"Think you'll need any more men?"

"No, but I'll want a car standing by ready to roll just in case."

"We'll spot two of them for you, one in Tillson's Garage, the other at the Servicenter. Ernie Bentley will drop an emergency kit in each under the seat."

"Got it," I said. "Now here's something . . . call Martin Grady and tell him Seaton Coleman and Porter Lockwood are on his back. They're considering lifting control from AmPet if this deal goes through. If it really looks rough I can stop these characters while they're here in the city. It won't be any nastier than what they're trying to pull, but a cute frame with a pretty blonde in a hotel bedroom will shut their mouths if it has to be like that."

"Better let Martin tackle it from the top. If it's necessary he'll pass the signal to go ahead. That pair are real spoilers."

"They're damn fools," I told him. "Look what they let Castro get away with."

"I'll get to him now. See you later."

When I hung up the operator rang me right back with a house call and a deep Midwestern drawl said, "Tiger?"

I waited until the identity code word came across, then grinned.

"Hi, Casey, come on up."

"Two minutes."

He was a big man, browned from the sun who seemed made to be lazy. Every move he made looked tired and when he sat he slumped, one leg over the arm of a chair. But Casey Ballanca was far from that. He was a graduate engineer who had worked his way up from a rigger in the Oklahoma oil fields to be chief research engineer for Grady. Not that he made it his main occupation though. He was in on section assignments as often as I was, the only stipulation in his contract with Grady. He liked excitement too.

He handed me a thick brown envelope, filled with type-written copy. "All the information on the AmPet process. If you get any queries you'll be able to answer without divulging anything essential, at the same time making them sure you know what it's about. Martin set up a beautiful cover for you and to all appearances you're an unknown but guiding genius behind the operation. Commit it to memory, then destroy the papers."

"It'll take a couple of hours."

"You're lucky to have that crazy memory of yours." He let me scan the sheets to get a general idea of the program and when I put them in my pocket said, "I saw the reports on Malcolm Turos in Newark. Somebody came across with the details of the *Gaspar Project* for a cool million in rubles. I'm going to put in a bid to get assigned to hitting that bunch if I can shake loose." He grinned at me. "I hope I see Turos again before you do."

"Again?"

"Sure, he was instructing in electrical engineering at the E.T.V. tech school I attended in Paris. Top man in his field, but his real purpose there was undermining the French Chamber of Deputies. That was when all the Commie trouble was going on. He pulled some beauties before they latched on to him and by then it was almost too late. The French smashed his play in time, but he got away."

"Why do you want him?"

"Because the bastard almost killed me. By accident I was in some remote bistro one night and saw him with a couple of men in some tight conversation. Hell, I didn't know they were Soviet agents, it was just one of those things, but he must have thought I was tailing him and later I left and a car damn near ran me down as I was crossing the street. It missed, but the guy at the wheel was Turos, all right. I was going to brace him on it but two days later he was gone with the French hard on his heels."

"You may see him yet."

Casey got up, stretched and walked in that somnolent manner to the door. "I'll be over at the Calvin if you want me for anything. Good late show tonight. Puts me to sleep."

"Okay. Thanks for the information."

"No trouble. If something comes up that you need filling in on give me a call. That's what I'm here for."

"Right."

I sat down, spread the sheets out and began pouring over them. What information I gathered had to be learned by rote and if I had to discuss it, would be mechanical in the delivery. At least the general scope would be accurate and anybody else would be sufficiently vague on the actual details not to be able to ask pointed questions.

Outside night settled on the city, a dirty, rainy night that hammered with annoying monotony at the windows, the wind breaking out into whistling sounds as it tore around the corners of the buildings. When I knew I had the material well fixed in my mind I touched a match to each sheet, let them crumple into a heap of black residue, then flushed it all down the toilet.

At seven o'clock I got dressed, cleaned and oiled the .45, loaded a couple of extra clips and snugged the gun down in its holster then slipped into my coat. When I was buttoning it up I saw the robin's egg-sized ruby lying where I had left it and for a long time I just stood there and stared at it.

No, it wasn't the ruby, it was something else. It was that thing in my mind again laughing at my attempts to snare it and bring it out into the open. I snapped the lamp off and the ruby lost its gleam, became, instead, almost purplish in color, and like that it had even more meaning still. The little voice laughed louder, challenging me to make the association that would win the game of hide-and-seek.

Something to do with Malcolm Turos, I knew. An oval ruby and Malcolm Turos. I picked it up, rolled it around in my palm searching for the connection, then, disgusted, dropped it in my side pocket, picked up my trench coat and hat, and left.

Anyway, it was going to be nice returning the gem. Maybe she'd let me put it back where I got it.

Even the rain didn't discourage the tourists that milled around in front of the Stacy. Royalty has its afficionados as well as movie stars, and even though the chance of a firsthand glimpse of a king was nearly impossible, there seemed to be something satisfying for the crowd in the proximity to what they considered greatness.

Again, the police were there in force, the Traffic Division keeping the cars moving, directing the limousines and taxis to the curb, the uniformed cops keeping the lanes open for the sidewalk traffic while making sure the arrivals had a clear passage to the hotel.

I skirted the area and used the side entrance, went in and up the steps to the desk, told the clerk I was going to the personnel office and found my harried friend busy sorting papers in the midst of jangling telephones. When I came in he threw up his hands, a pained look on his face. "Too much! Why can't we have a nice normal week? Why can't these idiots pick another hotel to disrupt?"

"What's the trouble?"

"Oh, the usual thing, the help bitching because they can't move without the police underfoot. Everything they do is inspected and they're treated like criminals. You know I had six people quit today? I'm lucky I took your offer and put those two fellows on. They're the only ones who don't seem bothered by all this mess. That little one is a wonder. I'd like to keep him."

"How did Teish go for the native dishes?"

"Raved about them, but I think they made everybody else sick. The chef couldn't stand those sheep's eyeballs staring at him. How can those people eat that stuff?"

"They don't know any better."

"Maybe, but get them over here awhile and their appetites change. I wouldn't want to pay their bill."

"You will, buddy . . . in taxes," I said. "Look, I want to speak to Harry and Lennie alone. Arrange it, will you?"

"No trouble." He took a key out of the drawer and tossed it to me. "There's a private locker room downstairs in back of the kitchen. Use that. I'll tell them to wait there for you."

"Thanks."

He smiled at me. "You're paying for it. I'm glad to be of service."

His call had gotten through before I reached the locker room and the two of them were waiting for me. Lennie had gotten used to his monkey suit and didn't look a bit uncomfortable in it at all. I unlocked the door, let them in, then closed and locked it again.

Lennie unhooked the recorder inside his jacket, handed it to me with the miniature speaker set up and I plugged the units together. "What do you have to report?"

"Open conferences. It looks like AmPet is in and there are plenty who don't like the idea. You're a main topic up there and everybody's wary because you're unknown to them. Believe me, there has been some fast researching done and you're going to be quizzed."

"I can handle it."

"No doubt. I picked up one bit," Lenny said seriously.

"They'll have some petroleum engineers on hand to try to rock you."

I grinned at him. "I'll have news for them."

"Let's hope I have news for you." He pointed his thumb at the recorder. "I left that thing in the serving tray when I laid out the spread for Teish and Sarim Shey. What garbage. Damn."

I turned the switch on, listened to the noisy rattle I guessed were dishes rattling, then the hum of voices filled the background. I could make out Lennie's voice, then pleased laughter of Teish El Abin and Sarim Shey who were surprised to find home so close and Lennie accepting their thanks.

Harry had bent close to the speaker and had he not been there I would have taken the sounds for unintelligible, overlapping conversation. He nodded silently, his dark face intent upon catching every word, and I didn't want to bother him.

Finally he said, "Sarim Shey is insisting it is poisoned—an American plot to kill the king and have an unobstructed inroad to Selachin's wealth." Then he grinned.

I said, "What's happening?"

"Teish has just asked him to taste everything first."

There seemed to be a two- or three-minute pause with only the deep murmur far in the back. Then there was more conversation and a gentle laugh.

Harry said, "Teish thinks it is funny. Sarim is obviously in good health and please not to eat it all. Sarim Shey made the appropriate remark that he was merely looking out for his king's safety and now they are eating."

I could hear the metallic clink of dish covers and the tinkle of the utensils. Occasionally Teish or Sarim would say something inconsequential in English to those present and what invitations they offered to others to join them were all politely refused.

Lennie chuckled and reached for a cigarette. "Couldn't blame them. The other waiters had regular sandwiches and drinks for them . . . if they could eat if after seeing that goo Harry dished out."

"Perhaps someday you will be hungry enough to eat even that, my friend." Harry told him. "I have eaten once even . . ."

"Don't tell me," Lennie said.

I stopped him there. Harry caught it and dropped his head down to catch the words. Twice I had to stop, rewind the spool and start it again to make sure he got it.

"Sarim Shey is telling Teish not to rush. They must go slowly. If he takes a loan of money from this country they will force him out."

"And Teish?" I asked.

"He does not say much. He listens carefully. Sarim wants time. Ah . . . wait. It is Teish now. He thinks the offer a good one. He can be a big king with power enough to be recognized through all the land. He does not care where the money comes from as long as it comes."

"And now it is Sarim . . . no, he says, the Americans wish his death. They will try to kill him because the Americans are greedy. Teish must listen to all offers, to consider carefully. He is a great leader and his people follow him religiously. To be a power he must . . ."

"What happened."

Harry grinned again. "Teish has just told him to shut up," he said.

There was no more after that. The spool had run out. I lifted it free, let Lennie insert another one and dropped it in my pocket. On the way upstairs I'd mail it to Charlie Corbinet with a note and let the boys at State listen to how much the lads from the hills were impressed with all their pomposity.

Lennie said, "What do you want me to do?"

"Both of you stay on the job. Teish might want another taste of his delicacies. Besides, pulling you out now might raise some eyebrows. Keep that recorder handy and use it if you get the chance. At least now we're sure which way Sarim is leaning. He's playing for time for some reason. Evidently Teish will do things on the spur of the moment and if he signs any deal with the U.S. too soon, Sarim's going to be damn unhappy." I stopped, thought back a bit and added, "By the way, did Sarim cut out solo any time?"

"Sure," Lenny said at once. "I was there picking up the dishes. He took out a cigar Teish objected violently to and told him to smoke it somewhere else. I saw Shey leave to go in the adjoining room, but he was back before I finished."

"He seem jumpy or anything?"

"Up until then he kept looking at his watch."

There was a phone in the corner and I called personnel and when I got my man said, "You know how many rooms are attached to Teish's suite?"

"Certainly. There were nine until this morning, then Mr. Shey requested that the small one on the end, not part of the complex, be added. The entrance is from another corridor aside from the room it adjoins. Why?"

"Is that service exit near it?"

"One moment." I heard him open a drawer, consult a chart, then: "Yes, immediately next to it, in fact. But that one is always locked. Is something wrong?"

"No, everything checks. Thanks." I hung up.

"What was that about?" Lennie asked.

"Sarim Shey made a contact outside earlier. Somehow he got a key to a service entrance which probably wasn't too difficult and slipped away a few minutes."

"Why?"

I shook my head. "I don't know. That cigar trick was planned. The damn door probably wasn't guarded because it was locked tight." I made a time check. It was almost eight o'clock. I tossed my hat and raincoat on the table and left them there. "Stay on tap. I'll get to you if I need you."

"Let's hope," Lennie grinned, his face happy with the prospect of some excitement.

But I had been in business too long. There were too many scars I could feel and some that hurt when it rained. "Let's hope not," I said.

This time I didn't have to be concerned about being admitted. There was a polite young guy at the desk waiting for me who should have worn his suit a little bigger because I could see the bulge of a gun at his hip. He told me Vey Locca had left instructions that I was to be escorted to her rooms immediately and pointed toward the elevator at the far end of the bank that stood there open, with the interior light off and only the folding gate across its opening.

As we walked over I turned my head idly toward the crowd surging around the other elevators, women and men in the finery that only an official occasion can bring out, waiting their turn to go up to the ballroom on the fifth floor.

There, smiling at me, so beautifully gowned, so damned gorgeous she was the absolute center of attraction for every man around her, was Rondine. Beside her was Talbot, man of the world and agent-at-large enjoying himself at my expense.

I got in the elevator and rode it up to Vey's floor.

She opened the door herself and as she did the music from the console in the living room faded in the way a movie would, coming from nowhere, but a perfect orchestral description to accentuate an unexpected moment.

I didn't know what I anticipated, but it wasn't this. Vey Locca had forsaken the Western world and now she was draped within the folds of startling white silk highlighted with odd, almost fluorescent overtones, that made her tawny skin and shimmering black hair vivid by contrast.

Nothing was concealed. Nothing was revealed, either, the fabric sweeping around her in such a manner that you knew she was naked within it because there was no need for anything else to be there. Every line and curve of her delightful body was possessed by the sheer cloth as it hugged her jealously, clutching the sensuous contours of her hips, grateful for the pleasure of enveloping her breasts. One shoulder was covered, the other bare, her waist encircled by an ingenious twist that was ropelike until it parted at the junction of her thighs and fell to curve in an opening down the side of her leg so that when she walked you had a titillating experience of seeing a glimpse of pure woman that was forbidden, yet ready to be received.

She knew what I was thinking. She realized the impact the sight of her had and enjoyed knowledge that desire was there in my eyes and the way I looked at her.

I grinned, knowing she was waiting for a compliment. "You'll be a sensation."

"I'm supposed to be," she said.

She was a little too cocksure of herself so I winked and said, "Come with me, little girl, and I'll give you candy."

For a second she lost her arched look, seemed puzzled, then broke into a gentle laugh. "Yankees," she said. "I will never understand you. I have gone to great lengths to be beautiful and you make silly jokes. Besides, I do not want candy."

"What do you want?"

In the living room she turned around and faced me. "You have something to return to me."

I picked the ruby out, looked at it again and felt that peculiar sensation of having an answer in my mind, then held it out to her.

The rich blossom of her mouth opened in a smile. "But aren't you going to put it back?"

"I was hoping you'd ask."

With my forefinger I touched the warmth of her belly, held the silken fold aside and thumbed the ruby in place. Beneath my fingers I felt her stomach undulate and the flesh around the stone encompass it, drawing it in, holding it there until it was firmly in place.

I had wondered and now I knew. Vey Locca waited for more, her senses matching mine, waiting for more regardless of the consequences, only I wasn't playing. There wasn't enough time.

"Shouldn't we go?"

Vey took my hand and led me to the bar. "I am a woman, my Tiger. Although Teish is the guest of honor I stand on my prerogative of making a late, but dramatic entrance. At the moment Teish is in the penthouse suite with members of your government. In exactly ten minutes he will be escorted down with Henry Balfour of your State Department and two policemen, make his appearance and a few minutes thereafter I shall follow, not late enough to disrupt or annoy anyone, but late enough to be observed. Do you mind?"

"Not a bit, kid," I said. "I hope Teish doesn't."

Her eyes had a sensual look, slanting upwards. "He favors you, Tiger. He would enjoy having a son like you. Perhaps he shall have."

I didn't answer. I wanted to tell her I could charge stud fees, but I didn't.

"Drink?"

"Four Roses and ginger."

She mixed mine and hers and we touched glasses. They were small and didn't take long to finish. Above the bar was an ornate clock and the minute hand was working its way into position. Vey put her glass down and held out her hand. "Come. It is time now. They will all be waiting." Then she added impishly, "But it will be me they see. The men, that is."

Damn broads are all alike.

We had the corridor to ourselves and walked to the bank of elevators alone. On this side there were four in a row and when I looked at the dials above the doors I noticed just the one on the end. Only it had a P after the twenty-sixth floor, the topmost level. As I watched it the pointer climbed from the lobby up through the numerals, passing us, until it slowed and rested at the penthouse apartment.

For a few minutes it remained there, then started its countdown, heading for the fifth floor. As it passed us I could hear the muted hiss of air and see the light of the car descending and muffled laughter behind the glass door.

Vey smiled, then reached out and pushed the downbutton for our elevator, timing her arrival at the ballroom like a stage pro coming out for a curtain call or the fight champ coming through the ropes last.

Inadvertently, I looked up at the dials. The others were still at ground level loading up, but the official car was nearing the fifth. I watched the pointer swing nearer the floor waiting for it to stop.

It never did.

Instead, it kept going down at that steady pace until it reached the main lobby and even then it didn't stop.

When it did the hand rested on the big B and I knew the car Teish was in had grounded at the basement and the hackles rose on the back of my neck like little fingers and the muscles of my neck stood out like thick cords.

I didn't realize our elevator had arrived until Vey took my arm. She was looking at me puzzled, said, "Tiger . . . ?" then I shoved her in ahead of me and told the operator to get moving and don't stop for anything. He assumed I meant not until the fifth floor and bypassed the other floors even though the red lights were blinking on his board, eased us in and pulled the door open at the fifth floor.

Vey stood there, knowing something was wrong, eyes wide with some unnamed fear. I gave her a push with my hand and she half stumbled out of the car.

"The basement . . . get some cops down there, damn it! Do it fast."

I nudged the operator with my fingertips. "Down. All the way and don't stop."

"Tiger!"

The door was closing, but I had time to yell, "They got Teish!"

It seemed like we crawled down, inch by inch. Through the glass partition in the door that was there for the operator to check his floors I could see the layers of steel and concrete. The numbers on the indicator over the door reversed themselves with agonizing slowness until we were at the mezzanine, then the lobby and finally the basement.

Before the door was all the way open I squeezed through, cut to the side where the other elevator had stopped and halted with my hands stretched to the walls of the car.

On the floor were three men sprawled in heaps, their bodies running blood, one with his hand still gripped around a service revolver that never left its holster and the other lying there with one hand clawing outward in a vain hope to grab a killer. The uniformed elevator operator still clutched the handle of his control trying to hold it in a stop position.

The other body was out on the concrete where he had crawled and from his formal attire I knew I had found Henry Balfour.

But there was no sign of Teish El Abin.

There was a sharp bend in the junction of the elevator wall and on the other side a steel door was still open leading to the street. The rain was running down the ramp and rivulets of water were just beginning to form at the bottom of it.

On the street normal traffic was passing by and the rainy mood of New York was not disturbed at all. I walked out and looked at the cabs passing by. Right by the curb was the glowing tip of a cigarette butt that the rain winked out as I looked at it.

Like the ruby when I turned the light off, I thought.

Upstairs a party was going on.

And someplace Malcolm Turos had Teish El Abin.

Teddy Tedesco had flashed the *Skyline* signal, all right. He didn't know how really right he was. Death on both sides of the world. We were dealing in death. I was in the middle again and the whole world was in a state of flux.

I looked at the dead cigarette on the curb.

Once more the little voice inside me laughed because I couldn't give it a name, but it held up the ruby as a hint and laughed again.

chapter 9

They held the interrogation in an empty room on the second floor, a dozen hard, cold faces staring into mine. Vey Locca had come down with Hal Randolph and some others from I.A.T.S. and had gotten me off the hook with her verification of my explanation, then was taken upstairs numbed by what had happened, but accepting the fact that nobody should know about it.

Two of the Washington men had come back in, drenched to the skin, flanking a scabby-looking character who had told them about a cab that he had seen pull to the curb, wait a few seconds, then pull away again. He didn't notice anything about it except that it was yellow like most of the others and he hadn't seen the driver or its occupants.

Just as he completed his story another cop came in with a phone message that a cabbie had been slugged and left unconscious in the back of a building off Ninety-second Street and Amsterdam and his cab stolen. There had been no attempt to lift his wallet that contained over sixty dollars and the guy who hit him was a passenger he was about to discharge at that address whose face he never got a clear look at. The license number of the cab was being flashed to all squad cars and the cab companies were alerting their drivers to be on the lookout for it.

Of the four men who had been shot, three were still alive but in critical condition. Only the elevator operator was dead, an innocuous little guy who had worked in the hotel since it had been built and had run the cars in the nine-story building that had formerly occupied the site. Two bullets had been recovered, imbedded in the walls of the elevator, both of .38

caliber, and the one taken from the operator matched them.

The initial concept was that the assassin was one person lying in wait in the basement with an accomplice outside, who had paid off the elevator operator to haul his passengers all the way down and had gotten killed for his trouble.

I was the only one who knew better.

When Charlie Corbinet came in I knew he had the picture of the situation and although it wasn't all clear yet, he knew I wasn't involved even though I was part of it. He walked over to where I was sitting and said, "You have anything to add?"

"Get Hal Randolph and let's go out to the elevator."

My old C.O. gave me that some old *"Okay, but watch yourself"* look I had seen so often and cornered Randolph, spoke to him a minute and nodded for me to follow them.

Outside the door Randolph said, "Don't you clear out, Tiger."

"Who's running?"

"So talk."

"Where was the elevator operator when you found him?" I asked.

"On the floor with the rest."

"Then he slipped."

Randolph gave me a hard, curious stare. "What are you getting at?"

I said, "When I saw him his hand was still holding the control down in the stop position. Has anybody tried to run this car since?"

He shook his head. "Why should they?"

"Suppose we try it, okay?"

Charlie said, "The lab boys finished?"

"Thirty minutes ago."

"So go along. Maybe there's an angle."

Hal Randolph stepped inside with me and Charlie behind him. I levered the door closed, shut the gate, and moved the control handle over into the UP slot. The car just stayed there. You couldn't even hear the whine of the electric motors. I pushed the reset button and tried again while they watched me. It still didn't move. Then I shoved the gate back and opened the door.

Randolph stood with his back to the wall, idly looking down at the dark stains on the floor at his feet. "What are you getting at, Tiger?"

"Get an electrical engineer to look at the circuits that activate this thing. They've been gimmicked by an expert. The operator couldn't stop the car at all. He went down where induced automation took him and died there. Take a look at the panel there." I pointed to the stainless steel face punctuated with buttons that indicated each floor. "This car can be operated automatically or manually and it wouldn't be a hard job for a first-class engineer to rerig the circuits."

Hal Randolph took his eyes off the floor and glanced up at me. They were small and hard and black. "Who, Tiger?"

"Malcolm Turos," I said. "He taught the course in a Paris Technical School. You might check out the possibility."

"Believe me, we will," he told me.

"You need me for anything?"

Charlie and Randolph looked at each other and Charlie said, "Keep everything under your hat. So far nobody knows about this and that's the way we want it."

"What are you telling those reporters upstairs?" I asked him.

"Teish El Abin is indisposed. The possibility isn't unlikely and they'll go along with it. We'll blame it on something he ate. In the meantime they have Sarim Shey and Vey Locca to stare at. She's putting on a good show for them. There's enough booze flowing to make the party a success and he won't be too much of a loss."

"Don't worry about it. Now . . . one question. Did Teish sign any agreements with our people before the snatch?"

Hal Randolph hesitated a second, then shook his head. "No. State was hoping to get something down tonight. Harry Balfour had the papers on his person. Now the whole deal is scrambled."

"Maybe. Okay, I'll be upstairs if you want to get hold of me."

"Stay out of the action," Randolph warned. "We don't need you in any part of this. Orders, Tiger."

I grinned back at him, waved to Charlie and got in the next elevator and told the operator to take me to the fifth floor. He waited for an acknowledgment from Randolph and when he got the nod, closed the door and took me upstairs.

The earlier formalities were finished with and most of the several hundred in the ballroom were on the dance floor with scattered groups at the tables. Over drinks the world's problems were being discussed, settled or agitated, and out of the affair would come a debriefing tomorrow that would fill hundreds of pages of reports.

I stood by the entrance scanning the crowd, saw Sarim Shey in earnest conversation with several of our government officials and as he talked, Vey Locca danced by, her partner a heavyset senator from an Eastern state. Sarim's glance was cold and there was a glitter of triumph in those dark eyes of his.

When I started circling the floor to the right I saw Rondine and Talbot walking back to their table and intercepted them. Although on the surface they appeared no different from the others, I knew they were tense from sitting on the powder keg that could cause a political explosion that would reach around the world.

"You filled in on the details?"

Rondine sat in the chair I held out for her. "As soon as it happened."

"Watch yourself," Talbot said. "We aren't the only ones who use lip readers."

I nodded, and sat with my back to the dance floor.

Talbot walked around behind me and leaned forward. "I have a few duties to attend to. Things have taken quite a messy turn, haven't they?"

"They'll get worse before they get better," I told him.

"By the way, just before you arrived one of our men said they found that stolen cab. It was left on lower Broadway, wiped nice and clean and not a witness around who saw anyone who was in it. They must have had another car waiting and switched into it. Right now they're conducting a house-to-house search, but I doubt if anything will come of it." He laid a hand on my shoulder. "See you later, old chap."

When he was gone I said, "Let's have it," and reached for her hand. Her fingers were cold as they tightened around mine.

"I was waiting for Vey Locca when she came in. Apparently she didn't know what had happened and was cool enough to make the best of it. I heard about it while she was upstairs and so did Sarim Shey. All of us were warned to keep quiet and Sarim was told the same thing. He put up quite a protest until one of your tougher men bluntly told him that if he—" she frowned, looking for the right words—"shot his mouth off he'd get tossed in the can." Rondine smiled at the thought and said, "He didn't have much choice and so far everything is all right. However, there are a couple of reporters who smelled something and went upstairs where they weren't admitted to Teish's suite. I think they suspect something."

"They'll keep the lid on if they're told to. You get near Vey at all?"

"Only once." She opened her bag and slid the compact over to me. "There were a few moments when Vey and Sarim Shey had a conversation that was in their own language and although they were both smiling outwardly I knew there was more to it than that. She was fuming about something."

"How do you know?"

Rondine squeezed my fingers. "Female intuition," she smiled. "Or perhaps no woman is that good an actress."

I took her by the arm. "Let's get out of here. I have a man downstairs who can unscramble their talk if it's on the tape."

She picked up her bag and we walked to the doors unhurriedly, Rondine stopping occasionally to speak a few words to people she knew. We got out in the lobby, picked our way through the milling crowd, went into the alcove that housed the offices and back toward the kitchen area. I found Lennie and Harry having a smoke near the locker room and waved them over, unlocked the door and let everybody get inside.

As briefly as I could I gave the details to Lennie while I was hooking the speaker up so he could get a report in to Newark Control for me. Right now we needed as many hands as we could get if Teish was to be found and Virgil Adams would have to get the word out immediately.

I looked at Harry. "Ready?"

He pulled out a chair and sat with his ear close to the gadget. I switched it on, picking up a babble of voices that were indistinguishable.

Rondine said, "I turned it on as I was walking toward them." Another voice in English came in then, and Rondine answered. "That's John Curtain from our embassy. He was my excuse for getting close to Vey and Sarim. I held my handbag so we wouldn't block out their conversation."

Harry looked up, alert. "I hear them now. Please . . . "

Impatiently we sat there while the spool unwound, watching Harry while he alternately frowned and nodded, a dark look of displeasure clouding his eyes. Although the voices were gibberish to me, he was getting the full import of them. A good five minutes passed before their conversation ended and Rondine said, "Vey left him at that point and Sarim was engaged by several gentlemen from Washington."

"What went on, Harry?"

"At first she told him what had happened. Sarim Shey immediately blamed it on the Americans. With all the precautions that had been taken, only they could have arranged for his disappearance. It wasn't at all likely someone else could have done it. He seemed certain that Teish would never be seen again alive."

"How did Vey take it?"

"Very angry, sir. She said that was what Sarim would like. He admitted that it would put him in an excellent position and he was going to take advantage of it. One thing he was going to do was see that she, Vey Locca, would have nothing to do in the affairs of state. In fact, he would personally see that she would never be admitted to Selachin again. In Teish's absence he would take over his powers and notify his capital that he was installing himself as temporary regent. Of course, with the money and powers he could wield, the position would soon become permanent. There were enough people in Selachin under his control who would see to that.

"Vey Locca used rather strong language, I'm afraid. She accused him of having a hand in the affair and Sarim did not seem disposed to deny it. In fact, she threatened his life, but Sarim laughed it off and told her that she would do better looking for protection for herself than attempting a murder. You were mentioned too, sir, rather disparagingly by Sarim."

"How?"

"To the effect that AmPet Corporation had better watch out for the competition now. That one does not like you, sir."

"Anything else?"

"Merely invectives, heated words. Those two are enemies. Sarim Shey does not intend to share his political advantage with any woman."

I put the recorder and speaker back in their kits and stuck them in my trench coat pocket that was lying there and turned to Lennie. "Get to Virgil with all of this, then take Rondine back to her apartment and stay there. Turos nailed his primary target but he won't leave without making a try for me. If I can, I'll make it easy for him to draw him out. He'll be lying low until the heat's off, but you never can tell."

"You think he's killed Teish?"

"Not yet," I told him. "It's easier to transport a live person than lug a dead body around. If they can make Teish think this was a plan rigged by us and let his oil fields go to the Soviets they might keep him alive. If they don't they'll knock him off in a hurry. They can work it either way and make it stick."

"Sarim Shey won't like that."

"He isn't dealing the cards, buddy. This bit's been masterminded in Moscow and Malcolm Turos is calling the turn on this end. The Reds aren't going to give a damn about him unless they decide to knock off Teish and let him in as a figurehead."

Rondine's hand touched my arm gently. Her eyes were worried although her voice didn't reflect it. "And what do you plan to do, Tiger?"

"Stay with Sarim Shey. He's in this deeper than it appears. It's beginning to make sense now when you figure out who gains by winning. I'm not playing Sarim down a bit. If he thinks he'll be edged out he'll make a move of his own. I want you out of the action completely. We have people covering your house and Lennie will be at hand. Turos knocked off one girl already to break even with me, but that won't satisfy him."

"I'll be careful. Please . . . you be too."

"At least I'm not on the outside looking in. What slight official capacity Randolph handed me takes the fuzz off my neck."

We split up there and I waited until the others had left before I went too. I dropped the keys to the locker room back in the office, took the elevator back to the fifth floor and got out. Charlie Corbinet and Hal Randolph were standing there watching me and when Randolph saw my coat said, "Going somewhere, Mann?"

"Back to the hotel. You know where I am."

"First you'd better come with us. We have some people anxious to talk to you."

I didn't want to lose the time, but I couldn't object without taking the chance of Randolph putting a stop on me. I took the bad with the good when I wanted a legal right to carry a rod in the state. I shrugged, followed their direction and went down the main corridor, then right to one of the smaller conference rooms where a pair of the young agency men lounged, relaxed but alert.

There were six of them there, two from I.A.T.S. that I knew by sight, a pair from the senate committee that had Martin Grady under investigation and two others I didn't recognize. One of the folders on the table had my name on it and was an inch thick. Another was Martin Grady's.

I waved to the group, was introduced without any hand-shaking and sat down. If they thought they had me worried they had the wrong guy. I had seen too many bluffs pulled and pulled too many myself to be bulldozed by closed dossiers and faces whose home was the courtroom. I let them know it when I said, "What can I do for you?"

The committee member drew his brows together and pulled the folder toward him. "We have a file on you, Mr. Mann. In fact . . ."

"So I see," I said easily, "but what can I do for you? This isn't a hearing and I don't see any subpoena with my name on it, so get to the point."

It rattled them, all right. I caught the exchange of glances, the *harrumps* of displeasure before he said, "Very well. From what we know about you I'll assume you are in possession of the facts that have transpired."

"Completely." I sat back and watched him, never letting my eyes shift off his.

"There have been certain AmPet Corporation stock transfers made recently and . . . "

"All very legal," I interrupted him.

"The value of these stocks was in excess of twenty million."

"Nice round sum," I said.

"Perhaps you'll be good enough to tell us where you got the money to purchase such a block of stock."

"Perhaps I won't be. Drop dead. What's next?"

"Now listen . . . "

Very easily I repeated, "Drop dead, or are you dumb as well as deaf?"

His face started to mottle and one of the I.A.T.S. men had to repress a grin. Charlie Corbinet was impassive, but his eyes were laughing at the guy's discomfort. I had him where the hair was short and he knew it.

Slowly, he let the anger fade, then looked up again. "Our government was about to enter into an agreement with that of Selachin. Teish El Abin stipulated AmPet as the organization he wanted to negotiate with and you in particular."

"Pretty nice of him, I'd say," I laughed.

"Don't be facetious, Mr. Mann. This is a delicate situation that can cause a shift in the balance of power in the Middle East. We know of your record and background. We certainly aren't going to allow any incompetent person to destroy our advantage here."

"I don't blame you," I told him.

"You know nothing of the oil recovery processes necessary to make development of those fields possible."

"Try me and see."

He nodded across the table to the thin gray-headed man who had never taken his eyes off me. "We intend to. Mr. Mac-Kinley here is with Dursto-Allied, a consultant in these matters. His company has been working along lines similar to AmPet, but admittedly is behind them. You may take an arrogant attitude at this time, Mr. Mann, but since you are at present bound by military orders we are in a position to curtail your activities completely. I want to see you get out of this one."

"You mean, if I don't measure up I'm being restricted?"

"Exactly. Very restricted. It will be very unpleasant . . . at least as unpleasant as we can make it."

"So go ahead and try me," I said.

He did. He took a full thirty minutes in objective discussion, digging, probing, feeling me out, trying hard to find the level of my knowledge. The others sat there bent forward, listening intently, but the subject was too technical and over their heads. I tried to stay ahead of his questions, my mind racing to recall the information I had pulled out of the report Casey Ballanca had prepared for me.

I did a damn good job. Halfway through the man was beginning to look worried, the doodles he was scratching on a pad becoming more complex each minute. When he tried for some points of research Casey had mentioned I merely grinned and shook my head. AmPet Corporation wasn't giving any secrets away to Dursto-Allied and he knew it. I stayed ahead of him every inch of the way and when he finished he stuck the pencil back in his pocket, his face drawn tight, and looked across the table.

"Well?"

The guy shrugged. "I'm afraid somebody has made a mistake. Mr. Mann seems well acquainted with the technical end. Even more so than I am." Then he looked at me shrewdly and added, "Though I wonder."

I stood up. "Is that all?"

Hell, there wasn't anything anybody could do except nod. I grinned at them again, collected my coat and hat and went outside with Charlie Corbinet. In the hall, away from the others, Charlie shook his head in amazement. "You can sure pull rabbits out of the hat, Tiger. How the hell do you do it?"

"I had a good teacher," I said, remembering back to the seminars he held in the old barracks building we had assigned to us.

"Sure, but I wonder who's doing the teaching now."

I left him at the elevator, checked my watch and went into the ballroom. There was still a crowd there hanging on to the last minute. I circled the place, looking at every face on the dance floor and at the tables, but the one I wanted wasn't there.

Sarim Shey was gone.

I knew I wouldn't get anything out of the agency men they had spotted around the hotel. They wouldn't give you the right time without a direct order from a superior, but I saw one face I knew and walked over to where Carl Jenner from the *Journal* was talking to Seaton Coleman. Every once in a while he'd jot down a note as Coleman rambled on, his deep voice heavy with authority, but sugared down for the press.

I motioned to Jenner that I wanted to see him and he cut Coleman off in the middle of a sentence, thanked him, and edged away to join me.

"Lousy party," he said. "What're you doing here, Tiger?"

"Nosy, I guess."

"You got any idea what's going on? Something stinks at this affair and I can't put my finger on it."

"You'll be getting a news flash with the rest when they're ready to give it to you."

His eyes lit up. "I though there was a hook in it. Care to give me a lead?"

"I'd like to, but I can't, but if I were you I'd stay on the street and follow any ambulances that are around. Incidentally, where's Sarim Shey?"

"That I'd like to know too. He disappeared a little while ago saying he was going to his room and nobody could track him down. The boys who were supposed to stay with him got one damn hot reading-off but they didn't have an explanation. What's your business with him?"

"Message to deliver."

"Good luck."

"Maybe he's with Vey Locca."

"Hell, she ducked out before he did." Jenner looked around speculatively. "Guess I'll take your advice and hop downstairs. Nothing more here." He gave me a knowing look. "If anything turns up, you know where to get me. One good turn always deserves another, buddy. I might come in handy some day."

"I won't forget you," I said.

The two cops were still on guard at Sarim Shey's suite and my identity papers with Army Intelligence came out and they scrutinized them. One cop said, "Nobody's inside. The others went through the place piece by piece."

"You see Shey come in?"

"We weren't on duty then. They had Feds covering the door. He came in and went out but somebody had their head up and looked and caught hell for it. Maybe he went to the World's Fair," he smiled.

"Well, I'll look around anyway."

"Go ahead."

Nobody had cleaned the suite up yet. There were still half-empty glasses around, whisky bottles on the bar and the ash trays full of butts. Every bedroom was loaded with fine luggage, the closets filled with clothes. Sarim Shey's room was directly opposite Teish's and a casual inspection of the place couldn't determine what was missing from his collection.

Getting out was easy enough. He simply went through the room he had used before and down the service entrance. *Why* he left was another thing entirely. I took a swing around his bedroom, pawed through the wastebasket cans, but apparently I hadn't been the first one there. A note pad on his dresser showed a few pages torn off, but no impressions were imprinted on the top page showing.

Nothing was in the desk drawers except hotel stationery and a ball-point pen. The blue desk blotter had a few inkstains and some squiggly lines where somebody had scrawled to get a ball-point pen writing. Outside a faint outline of oblong blocks there were no other indentations in the soft paper.

I started away, stopped and turned back to look at the

markings again. There was something familiar about them. It took a few minutes to make sense, then I got it. There were six blocks. The right-hand one had an X drawn through it. Outside in the corridor were six elevators. Teish El Abin had come down in the one on the far right.

Sarim Shey had gotten a diagram of the route Teish was to use under guard to get to the ballroom and Sarim had passed on the information in time for the elevator to be gimmicked.

So the bastard was in it up to his ears after all.

And he wouldn't want Teish alive. Even if Teish kicked the deal and went to the Commies, Sarim Shey would still be a stooge, always second in command and not the powerhouse he wanted to be. He didn't want to have to outlive Teish and couldn't take a chance on having a successor oust him completely. He couldn't afford to have Vey Locca in an advisory capacity either. With Teish dead she had no importance. With Teish alive she could point the finger right at him.

So Sarim Shey had to contact Malcolm Turos. One way or another he had to convince him Teish had to be knocked off. The only thing that could save Teish was his ultimate importance in the Soviet scheme of things, and it was Malcolm Turos who would make that decision.

And if Teish died, so did Teddy Tedesco and Pete Moore. Every hour made their chances of survival more slim.

I tried the door Sarim had used leading to the extra room on the end of the suite. It was locked, but three hard raps with my heel tore the metal loose from the wood and the door flew back. Light from the bedroom behind me threw a glow inside and I saw the lamp on the dresser and switched it on. I walked past the beds, stopped, and looked down between them.

Vey Locca lay sprawled out face down, her clothes torn, hair spilled forward over her head and a small pool of blood spreading under her body. I turned her head, feeling my face grimace at the sight of the ugly blue welts that discolored her jaw and eye.

But she wasn't dead! Damn, she had been left there to die and she was still alive!

I rolled her over and saw the hilt of a stiletto, a wicked thin-handled thing that was made to deliver death at one blow, sticking from her belly and when I ripped away the cloth from around it I saw why she was still alive.

When the blade was driven into her belly it hit the ruby in her navel and was deflected sideways into the flesh and muscle of her stomach without the killer realizing what had happened. She lay there unconscious from the beating she took on her face and from shock of the wound, but she was alive.

She couldn't hear me, but I touched her face and said,

"You'll be okay, baby," then picked up the ruby and dropped it in my pocket.

I didn't want anybody to stop me. I didn't want to have to deliver any explanations. I went out, spoke to the cops a minute, then took the elevator down to the lobby. I made my call from there. It took a couple of minutes to locate Charlie Corbinet upstairs and when he came on I said, "Tiger, Charlie."

"Where are you?"

"Across town," I lied. "Listen . . . check the room adjacent to Sarim Shey's. Vey Locca's there and she's hurt. She was supposed to have died but it didn't work out. She's unconscious now and when she comes around she ought to have a story for you. But, damn it, keep her under cover. If word gets out she's still alive somebody will get to her."

"Tiger . . . "

I didn't hear the rest. I hung up, but I was thinking back to the room and the telephone on the nightstand between the two beds. The phone was almost on the edge of the table where somebody had used it, not where it normally would be.

My identity papers bought me the information. The operator at the PBX board looked up her charge calls and found the only one credited to that room. It had been made that evening to a number she wrote down and handed to me. I didn't want to hang around so went out to the street and looked around for a gin mill that would have a pay phone.

It was still raining. It always rained on nights like this.

I headed west, picked a bar a block away and called Virgil Adams, asking for a reverse on the number. He went through his listings and found the address that went with the phone number that had been called.

Then I felt like slamming my fist through a wall. When I got there it was a public pay booth on a corner of Tenth Avenue and the gas station behind it was closed. The phone had been used as a contact point and nothing more.

I called Virgil Adams back, gave him the information and asked if any of our informants had come up with anything. Several false leads had been tracked down and found to be negative and the best we could hope for was a little luck coming from the manager of a belly dance joint like the Turkish Gardens who remembered seeing a person answering the description of Malcolm Turos as he had looked the night I spotted him.

He had changed a five-hundred-dollar bill when he paid his check for a meal and drinks and the manager had noticed a card in his wallet from a club owned by his friend, Stephen Pelloni. Virgil had placed two men and a female operative in the place in case he showed again.

Virgil was about to sign off when he said, "Hold it, Tiger. Just got a note."

"What is it?"

"A little oddball, but it's from one of our sources. The guy has a used clothing place on the East Side." He rattled off the address and I memorized it. "Something about a man with a strange voice buying a very small-sized suit of old clothes. His boy happened to look in the car outside and saw a man there in what looked like a nightgown to him. What do you think?"

"May have something, Virg. I'll get over there."

"The guy makes ten grand if he comes through."

"We'll know soon enough."

The taxi dropped me off on the end of the block and I walked the rest of the way. During the day the street would teem with people and pushcarts, but now it was almost deserted. A couple of bars were still open, a restaurant had a few people in it, but the blinds were drawn on the door and the lone waiter inside was standing beside it, arms crossed as he waited for everybody to go home.

Halfway down I found the address I was looking for, a run-down place that had a window full of odds and ends and a sign, WE BUY OLD CLOTHES, over the doors, with *Leo Rubin, prop.* under it. There was a night light on in the back of the place, but no one inside. I checked the door next to the store and flicked a match on to read the names under the doorbell.

The lower one had *Rubin* scratched in the metal and I pushed the buzzer. Nobody answered so I stood there with my finger on it until I heard a door slam upstairs and a voice yelled down the stairwell, "Yes, yes, what is it? Don't you know what time it is? A man is to sleep at this hour. Now what do you want?"

"To give you ten thousand bucks maybe," I called up.

"So it is not too late for a little work then. Upstairs. Come upstairs and watch out for the junk on the stairs. These kids . . . junk all over everyplace. There is no light."

I picked my way up, toeing toys and boxes out of the way until I reached the landing. Framed in the light from his door was a withered man of indeterminate age wrapped tightly in a bathrobe, peering at me from behind heavy-lensed glasses, his face squinted up trying to make me out in the darkness.

"Now who are you, please? Who is it that wants to give me so much money?"

"Does the amount ring a bell?"

"I have heard such a sum mentioned."

"And you reported about seeing a man with a strange voice."

He stopped squinting then and looked around the darkness uneasily. "Come in, come in. It is not right to talk about such things in public."

"Anyone live upstairs?"

"Only mice. It is a storeroom for me and sometimes a place to put the relatives who you don't want to visit too long." He stepped aside and waved me through the door.

From one side a voice thick with the accent of the Lower East Side said, "Who is it, Leo? If it is those card players tell them that they should go home where they belong."

"Be quiet!" Rubin said sharply. "This is business for men." Obviously he was the head of the house because the woman shut up and didn't say another thing. "In here, the kitchen," he told me. He went to the cupboard, took down two glasses and a dusty bottle. "It is the custom here. First the wine, then the business. After the wine I can tell if a man speaks truthfully."

I dumped mine down in a hurry, anxious to get with it, but some types you can't push and he was one. When he was ready he sat down, pointed to a chair for me, folded his fingers inside one another and waited. "My name is Mann," I said, "Tiger Mann. We have people looking for a certain person with an odd voice."

"Who is this one, please?"

"Nobody you need know. He's a killer and he's ready to kill again if it eases your conscience any. We have to nail him before it happens. Now you tell me what you saw, when and how. All the details."

He nodded, took off his glasses and wiped them, then adjusted them back on carefully. "It was the little one they call Dog who has told us to watch for this person. So for that much money, everyone is watching. Once Dog himself was paid generously for giving information and we know this. Once I myself was given a tidy sum for letting someone know what I found in the pocket of a suit that was stolen and later sold to me. Yes, I know how you people work, so I am watching.

"It is tonight and I am finishing repairing several old garments for sale when this man came in. Naturally, I first notice his clothes and they are not in need of replacement."

"Describe him?"

Leo Rubin made a peculiar face and spread his hands out in a gesture as he shrugged. "So nothing special. A man. Maybe forty. Not big, not small."

"Average?" I probed.

"Yes," he agreed at once. "Like so. It is hard to describe him. His suit, that I can tell you. Dark gray, not too old, but it is not an American suit. There are differences only an expert can tell," he said proudly. "Glasses and a hat he wore and good shoes with rubber soles. Why he wants to buy in my store is a curious thing." He shrugged again and made another gesture with his hands. "But who knows people? Sometimes they see a bum, they buy him a suit, the bum sells it right back to me for less and drinks down the street. We all make a little bit then."

"The guy. Tell me about him."

"So I am telling you. It is when he talks that I notice this. It is like he is having a hard time to talk and all the time he keeps his chin down, like so." He demonstrated it for me, then looked up. "At first I forgot about what Dog has told me because I am trying to understand him. He wants a suit, size thirty-four, any color, any style. Just a suit and I feel bad because I do not think I have any that small in stock without going upstairs to the storeroom. So I look anyway and I find a suit. For five dollars I sell it, not in a wrapping even. He takes it over his arm and leaves. Outside he is in a car. He goes away."

"What kind of a car?"

"So who can tell? It is raining and I do not go out to look. My boy comes in then and he tells me that inside the car is a man in a nightshirt. A white one. I think then and call Dog and tell him about the one with the voice that can't talk and he tells me later he has made a phone call and has let somebody know about it. Then you come." He looked at me hopefully. "Is it enough?"

"No."

His face fell with regret.

"I have to know about that damn car."

"That I cannot tell you."

I was going to stop right there and not waste any more time, but a piping voice from the doorway of the kitchen said, "I can tell, Papa."

"You can tell nothing. Go to bed," Rubin commanded.

"Wait a minute."

"What do these boys know?" he insisted. "They . . . "

"How old are you?" I asked the kid.

"Eleven. And it was a black Chevy sedan, a 1963 model."

"And you saw a guy in a nightshirt in the back?"

He nodded. "Sure. I even jumped so I could look through the back window. Some old guy. He looked sick."

I tried for the impossible. "You get a look at the plates?"

"Naw." The kid shook his head.

"See," Rubin said, "what do these kids know? They see nothing and . . . "

"But I know whose car it was," the kid grinned.

The feeling was there. I felt good all over, a wild, crazy

good and knew I had hold of something. I said, "Whose?"

For a second the kid hesitated, a sly look on his face, then Rubin said in a voice that was going to tolerate no nonsense, "Say your piece."

"Yamu Gorkey's." I waited, watching him, and he added, "He's got that loan place down on Fulton."

Leo Rubin stood up, his face stern. "You have been so far from home?"

"Aw, Pop."

Rubin took his glasses off again, worked the earpieces, put them on and said. "That Gorkey is a bummer. A real bummer. He is a Communist and a bummer."

"How do *you* know him, Pop?" the kid chuckled.

"I know from the people he takes," Rubin exploded. "You are not to go near Fulton, do you hear? I am telling you . . . "

"How did you recognize his car?" I asked the kid.

"Last week on the back somebody scratched *Yamu stinks*. I seen it there. Besides, I'm sure some way else."

"Spill it," I said.

"Yamu was driving, that's how I'm sure."

"Where does he live?"

"Upstairs over Sloan's Bar four blocks from here. That's the big one in the middle. Got about six on that block. The Greenies . . . that's a social club . . . they're havin' a party tonight and that block's jumpin'. Boy!"

"To have seen such things. To think such a young boy . . . Mr. Mann, it makes me afraid."

I pulled a five-dollar bill out and held it out to the kid. He grabbed it eagerly and folded it up in his palm. "You earned it. Just don't talk it up."

"What do I care? That Yamu Gorkey does stink. He's always taking a poke at us."

"To bed!" Rubin said, arm outstretched, his finger pointing. The kid grinned again and ran off. When Rubin looked at me with another shrug he shook his head. "They are so different."

"Maybe he just got you a wad of dough, Mr. Rubin."

"Perhaps. Is it worth what they have to see?"

"In this case it is," I said.

chapter 10

The kid knew what he was talking about when he said the block was jumping. Every bar and store on the stretch between the two avenues sported bright orange placards with blazing lettering announcing this as the Greenie's annual social week and listed events coming up with everything from a softball game in Central Park to beer barrel rolling down the street. This was their opening night and from the friendly blasts they got from stickers plastered on the walls and poles from the other clubs, they had plenty of rivals for competition.

All six bars were wide open and blaring jukebox music and what crowd wasn't packed inside was going from one place to another. Everybody had half a jag on and paid no attention to the rain. One guy was sprawled up against a parked car, out like a light, and further down two more were getting sick at the curb. One finished chucking his cookies and turned back into the bar again. Like a seagull, I thought.

I looked at them all with a nice happy grin because if they hadn't been there it wouldn't have been necessary for Turos to buy clothes to wrap Teish in. He would have stuck out like a sore thumb in his native dress he was wearing, but in a nonde-script suit, propped between a couple of guys, he was just an-other character who had belted too many and was paying for it and his friends were carrying him home.

Sloan's was the hit spot, all right. They had a three-piece band hammering away instead of a juke and the B girls were making theirs at the bar. A couple of hustlers were trying to make a buck, hitting the guys who came out of the place, but right then they were more for the beer and booze than they were for the broads and waved them off with a "later maybe" sign.

One of the dames spotted me, got the drop by cutting in front of her friend and swung over, her legs flashing whitely under the belted black plastic raincoat. The pert little hat she wore was soaked through, but it didn't dampen her spirits any.

She smiled broadly, her pocketbook swinging from her shoulder and said, "Going places tonight?"

Then she got up close where she could see my face and the smile became a little forced. She was tabbing me for the fuzz and could see herself in the cooler already. I didn't want to shake her illusions. Sometimes you could play it right and come out winning, even with that type. "Relax, kid," I told her. "No roust. Vice can handle their own business."

The smile got friendly again. "They told Buddy not to pull that gun on Gretch. Somebody called in, eh?"

"You know these socials."

The broad got friendly cute then. "You ain't gonna pop 'em are you?"

I shook my head. "Nope. As long as it's peaceful, let them have fun."

"Huh, with all the squad cars rollin' by nobody's messin' around. It ain't like last year."

"You seen Yamu Gorkey?"

"That punk?" She made a face of disgust. "He needs more nudgin' than he gets to stay in line. He's probably upstairs countin' his dough, the Commie bastard. Always talking it up with the jerks who don't know better. You know how many May Day parades he was in?"

"We know."

"Sure, and you let him run that racket of his. Why don't you roust him?"

"Better than standing in the wet," I said.

"He went upstairs a long time ago. Shake him up good."

I winked at her, let her walk back to her friend and went over to the door that led to the apartments over the gin mill. Parked directly opposite the building was a black 1963 Chevy sedan. I didn't have to look at the sign scratched on the back to know whose it was.

The outside door opened into a small vestibule and the inside one was locked. All it took was a plastic credit card slipped into the slight space between the door and the jamb to force the beveled tongue back and the door opened easily. I closed it behind me, letting the lock fall in place quietly, then took out the .45 and cocked the hammer back.

Old carpeting ran up the stairs, muffling my steps, but I

stayed near the junction of the wall to avoid making them creak. I took them two at a time, but slowly, and once when one let out an ominous groan, stopped and waited to see if the sound was heard. There was only one light in the place and that was behind me, so that if anybody jumped me I was going to be a beautiful target. Ahead all was wrapped in the dusky gloom of shadows I couldn't see through at all, a perfect place for an ambush.

A good five minutes passed before I reached the top, then stood there trying to make my eyes adjust to the darkness. I couldn't hurry, yet I couldn't afford to wait. When I thought I was ready I felt my way along the wall, touched a door and paused there. My fingers felt a padlock snapped into a hasp and I debated blasting it open, but if I was wrong it would only alert anyone waiting. I felt the gossamer touch of a spider-web then and grinned because the luck was still there. That was one door not used recently.

I had to run my hand along the banister until I came to the bend in the stairs going up, then took those steps the way I had the others. Only this time I didn't have to be quite so careful. From the landing above I could hear the distant sound of a television, the theme music of a popular program and the voice of an announcer running through a beer commercial.

Then I was there.

The door was a wood panel job, the lock a fine new Yale, but the house was old and the framing around the door warped enough so that even the precaution of a massive lock was insufficient. The plastic credit card got the latch back again and I twisted the knob so that the door opened about four inches.

No more. A chain was strung across the opening and through the angular inch-wide gap I could see a pair of crossed legs cut off by a wall where somebody was very nice and comfortable watching his favorite show.

I had two choices. I could put a shot through the legs then try to break the lock out of the wood or shoot the damn thing off and get in there as fast as I could. The trouble was that with the odds at stake, one second's delay would give anyone inside a chance to grab a gun and even the odds up . . . or drop a slug into Teish. If he was there.

And it was a chance I couldn't take.

But I got my third choice when I looked at the chain carefully. Those things are supposed to be strung up in a way so that any opening of the door at all automatically slides the stop in a position. It was designed so that the door had to be fully closed first before it could be unhooked, but in this age of do-it-yourself gadgetry too many people tried doing things their own way without reading the directions first and made mistakes. Yamu Gorkey made a beauty.

He left slack in the chain.

All I had to do was close the door almost shut, use the tip of my pen to reach in and slide the catch back out of its holder, and the chain swung down across the door with a metallic click and I walked on inside. The legs were still crossed, keeping time to the rugged beat of the theme music.

Yamu Gorkey was a big, wide-faced guy with scars over both eyebrows and lips twisted in a perpetual sneer even when he was enjoying himself. He sat there in his shirt-sleeves, hands folded across his belly, his expression mirroring the action on the TV screen. Unlike the outside of the building, the apartment was ornate, from the biggest color TV available to the expensive furniture that was shoved with lousy taste in any place it would fit. Jammed in a corner were three filing cabinets and the office desk next to it was loaded with papers and account books. Yamu Gorkey ran his operation out of his house as well as his office.

I stood there thirty seconds before he saw me, and when he did his face become loose and flabby and for the first time his sneer dissolved into a look of fear. It was too sudden, too quiet. The gun was too big and just my standing there was enough to give him the wild shakes without a word being said.

His mouth hung open and he swallowed hard, finally saying, "What the hell . . ."

"Teish," I said. "Where is he?"

Somehow they all do the same thing. They think they have the edge because you don't shoot first and ask questions later. They grab the odds because they know that they have no conscience and when death is the perfect answer, they can produce it. Everybody else is a patsy to be taken and when you have them in your own back yard you can even get away with it in a court of law. They know that the right guys won't move until the wrong ones make the first move and by then the wrong ones are right because the other ones are dead.

So he got that look on his face and I wanted to tell him what kind of a mistake he was making and he didn't give me a chance. He had the gun wedged in the chair beside him where it wasn't supposed to be seen and it was only when he had it in his mitt and pointed at me that he knew he had made the big mistake, the one-of-a-kind type, and tried to scream for me to stop even as he pulled the trigger of his gun.

The slug caught me in the left side with an impact that half twisted me around. Behind me I heard something break from where it had gone on through, smashing into glass, but by then it didn't matter. Yamu Gorkey had no top of his head and was going backwards over his chair to lie in a ridiculous heap on the floor, a corpse that was too dead to bleed.

On television, the announcer came on and talked about beer some more.

I opened my coat, looked at the hole in my shirt turning red and felt the passage of the bullet. It had gone through the fleshy section between my ribs and hip, almost painless at the moment, but in a little while I'd be hurting. I stayed flattened back against the wall, protected by the angle of it. No other slugs came at me; there was no sound except the television, the rain and occasionally a yell from the street below.

I left Gorkey where he was, pushed through the other rooms until I came to the bedroom at the back of the building. Every time I opened a door I expected another gun to blast out of the darkness and was ready for it, but none came.

Then there was Teish El Abin, a pitiful little guy lying trussed up on a bed, spreadeagled so that his arms and ankles could be lashed to the metal framework, a gag stuffed into his mouth. His eyes were wide with some terrifying fear, not knowing who I was, but seeing the shape of me silhouetted there with the .45 in my hand.

I yanked the gag out of his mouth and cut him loose before he recognized me. If I thought there would be thanks, I was wrong. All his Eastern wariness came back to him in an expression of absolute disdain and he said, "Your game has gone far enough, Mr. Mann." He was exhausted, frightened and old, but he had to tell me.

I jerked him out of bed and led him stumbling into the front room. Even the sight of the body on the floor didn't seem to alter his attitude any at all. He sat down, slumping there, watching me. "It will do you no good." He waved his hand toward the floor without looking at what was left of Yamu Gorkey. "Do you not think that in my time I have . . . arranged such a scene?"

I got sore then. He was still a gook in my country and he wasn't handling me like that at all. He was begging, we weren't asking. He came over here with his hand out and something to sell, but he didn't own the world. He controlled only a tiny chunk of it that was good if we managed it for him. "You were suckered, old boy. You were jostled by the Soviets and they wanted you to think it was an American plot."

Teish nodded toward the body. "He is an American?"

"Maybe by birth."

"And the other one?"

"A Red agent."

"Ah, no. He spoke the language well. Too well."

"You aren't that astute, Teish. Languages are easy to come

by. The other one was Malcolm Turos."

His eyes were red rimmed, hating me, thinking of how he had offered me Vey Locca up on a platter. "You may kill me, but I know what I know."

Well, screw him. I opened up my coat. The bloodstain had damn near encircled my waist. "I don't take a hit for anybody," I said, making sure he could see it.

His gesture was vague, but adamant. "Nothing. Self-inflicted wounds have many uses. They take a man from a battlefield. They are points of proof to minds not used to such things."

I grinned at the little mutt sitting there defying me. Age had certain advantages and he was taking his for all it was worth. But I still had a hole card. I took the recorder and the speaker rig out of my pocket and plugged them together. I let it run and let him hear Vey and Sarim Shey in conversation together and when it had run through the spool I said, "You're in the wrong league, old man."

There was no fear in his eyes any longer. Simply fatigue, and when he looked up at me I saw the hurt there, the soft anger at what had been done to him, the hidden implications, the self-promises of what would happen if he could be in control again and he said, "I am sorry, Mr. Mann. After what I have said to you the insult can only be paid for with my life and that you have in your hands."

He sat there waiting. Had it been the other way around he would have killed me.

I said, "There are two men in Selachin. Our men. One is Teddy Tedesco, the other Peter Moore. At present they are being hunted down in the hills by your people, led by the same ones who tried . . . this."

"Yes?"

There was a phone on the table next to him. "Stop them. I want them back alive. They are my friends."

"It is enough?"

"It is enough," I said.

And a phone call went through on Yamu Gorkey's phone bill that he would never be able to pay. It followed the Atlantic path, was transmitted through relay stations and was probably intercepted along the line, but it didn't make any difference. In thirty minutes Teish El Abin had reached his palace and his words were direct and forceful. He spoke for five minutes before he hung up, then nodded solemnly to me. "It is done."

"Almost," I said. I picked up the phone and called Virgil Adams. I got the report in and when I told him Teddy and Pete were off the hook he couldn't say anything for a minute. He caught the sharp corners in my tone then.

"You okay, Tiger?"

"Hit."

"Bad?"

"No. I'll stay on it."

"Don't be a fool. You got Lennie there and Casey Ballanca standing by. Pitch it at them."

"I have a personal interest in the business, buddy," I said, then cradled the receiver.

Teish was watching me with new interest, a peculiar expression lighting his eyes. I dialed Charlie Corbinet's number, let it ring four times before he got on. I said, "I have Teish, Charlie."

I could hear him scramble to his feet. "Where?"

"In an apartment over Sloan's Bar," I told him and gave him the address. "How's Vey?"

When I mentioned her name, Teish hands went white around the arms of his chair. Charlie said, "Conscious, but not talking. She'll be all right. She won't talk to anybody but you. It looks like you have everybody over a barrel."

"Martin Grady ought to be in the catbird seat then."

"He is, Tiger. They're calling off that congressional investigation for the time being. The heat's too much for them. Nobody seems to know how the hell you worked it, but they aren't asking any questions. We'll get our people right up there. You better get ready for a session with Hal Randolph."

"I won't be here, Colonel."

"Look . . . "

"Malcolm Turos is still loose. He lost his main target but he still has a secondary one. Me."

I hung up, swung around to Teish who was sitting there quietly, waiting to hear what I had to say. I gave it to him, briefly, but in detail. When I finished he nodded, his dark eyes boring right through me. "I will have a son like you," he said. "One way or another, he will be like you."

I didn't answer him. I picked a handkerchief out of my pocket and jammed it under my shirt over the bullet hole. It was just beginning to hurt. Through the rain and the noise below I heard the whine of sirens coming closer. I belted the coat around me and stuck my hands in the pockets.

Under my fingers I could feel the ruby.

There was something smoothly sensual about it and when I touched it that little figure came out in my mind again, laughing at me. He danced closer and closer to the front and there was enough light on him for the first time and I knew he wouldn't get away. I had a good look that time and knew that it was tied in with the ruby and if I thought on it I'd give him a name and he'd be gone forever.

The sirens were louder now and people were running into the street. "They'll be here in a minute. You'll be all right now."

Teish nodded again, slowly. "Everything will be all right," he said, his words filled with meaning.

I went down the stairs, stood across the street until the squad cars and the unmarked ones pulled up in front of the buildings, then crossed over before they could get the street cordoned off and started walking aimlessly, head down into the rain and smelling the air.

My fingers were wrapped around the ruby in my pocket.

There are nights when you can have the city to yourself. The rain drives those who inhabit it further into the recesses of the buildings, away from the veins and arteries that connect its vast parts. Where I walked was like an amputated member of a body, a ghost town that had been alive only hours before.

Overhead thunder rumbled and the rain came in waves of stinging needles, challenging my right to be there. Both sides of the street were flanked with aged masonry that soaked the rain into its pores, thirsty for anything that was life-giving. Their windows were dirty on the inside, blank. The wetness liberated smells that had been trampled into the pavement until the air was filled with the odor of commerce, green smells, sea smells, machine smells and the hint of sweating men who had left their spoor behind.

I was alone there, but somewhere in the city was Malcolm Turos and a pig named Sarim Shey. In my pocket was the key that could unlock the door to their secret room so that I could go through and while I walked I fingered the blood-red thing that had rested so ably in the dimpled navel of a beautiful woman.

What was it like? I thought. A ruby. Oval-shaped and thick through the middle. It wasn't the appearance of it that mattered—I knew that. It was the shape. It reminded me of something that had been said—words that slipped from a tongue, never remembered by the person who had said them, but they were there, formed into a little dervish in my brain.

He was laughing at me again.

I laughed back.

In a little while, I thought, *it will come. Laugh while you can because when I remember you'll disappear like a puff of smoke.*

A ruby . . . a marble? No, that wasn't it. The damn thing wasn't very big at all. If I didn't know what it was I'd take it for a nut somebody had rubbed smooth.

I stopped, because the little dervish stopped too and was looking at me with bright eyes aghast at the thought that he had been recognized, then tried a crazy dance again to dissuade me from my trend of reasoning.

A nut. I said it to myself, then again aloud. Who had mentioned nuts?

The dervish was going mad now and I knew that I had him.

Harry had said it. Malcolm Turos said he didn't like the city because he couldn't stand the smell of litchi nuts.

And the little dervish disappeared in a puff of smoke like I knew he would.

I left the end of the city that was the amputated part and walked back toward the lights until I saw the avenue where the life of it flowed. My side was a burning ache that throbbed constantly and I knew whatever I had to do had to be done soon and when I reached the intersection I stood on the corner and waited twenty minutes until a cab cruised by, coming back to Manhattan from taking a fare across the bridge to Brooklyn.

I didn't want to get involved with explanations, and outside of a few slobs who worked the TWA section of the Kennedy Airport, New York cabbies were the best when you put it to them right. I hung a ten-dollar bill from the Martin Grady fund over the back of the seat, watched it picked out of my fingers and said, "Find me a Chinese laundry."

He met my eyes in the mirror, trying to see if I was a kook or not, decided I had something going, then pulled away from the curb, scouting both sides of the street for what I wanted. When he ran out of possibles on one street he tried another, crisscrossing the city patiently.

One thing you can say about the Chinese who work the laundry business—they're ambitious. They never seem to sleep. Sometimes you think they work in shifts, but it's always the same guy at the ironing board no matter what time you go by his place.

The one we found was named George Tung and he was downstairs in a brownstone in the upper Forties blowing spray through his water pipe, hot irons cooking over a gas flame while a radio was piping in soft music from a local station.

I got out of the cab, said, "Wait for me," and handed the driver another ten. He liked the action and lit up a smoke.

George Tung was a brown little man full of smiles and when I walked in lit up like a birthday cake. The talk was coming hard now, the gnawing pain in my side cutting off my breath.

"Yes? You want laundry?" They have great memories, the Chinese. He knew damn well I had never been there before.

Instead of trying to talk I laid another ten on the counter. He looked at the bill, then me, smiling, but not understanding and his mind reading me off for a hophead or something in strange characters. I pushed the bill his way. "Litchi nuts . . . where do you buy them?"

His head bobbed up, his eyes round over his smile. "I do not buy. Don't like. I give something else." He reached under the counter and threw a calendar at me with a naked blonde on the front of it.

"Who sells them?"

"You buy litchi nut?"

"No, I want to know who sells them."

"You go Chinatown?"

"No."

"That's good. They don't sell there."

There was one way to stop him. I reached out to take the ten bucks back and he put his thumb on it. "James Harvey, he sell."

"He's not Chinese."

"Mother," he said.

"Got a phone book?"

His head bobbed again and he added, "James Harvey my cousin. Have many cousin. He sell next to Flood Warehouse. You know where is? James live in fine house 'way uptown. Tomorrow you buy and I tell him you come, okay?"

"Sure. You do that."

"You want litchi nut now?"

I started to turn away. "No." He was still looking at me like I was a nut too. "Any other places?"

"My cousin biggest. Ask anybody. Tom Lee Foy has place not far from James. He sell. He have fine house too 'way uptown. You know Flood Warehouse?"

"I know Flood Warehouse," I said.

When I reached the door he chuckled. "Bring laundry to George Tung. Do fine job. Very neat, not much starch."

"You got enough," I said.

The cabbie flicked his cigarette out the window when I got in. "Where to now?"

"Flood Warehouse. You know where it is?"

I got the eyes in the mirror again. "Yeah, I know where it is."

"Then let's roll." I sat back against the cushions and closed my eyes. I could feel the wetness seeping around my middle and wondered just how bad the thing in my side was. I had to get to a doctor and there just wasn't that much time. I hated to give away any odds at all, and with a person like Turos that was all the edge he needed. I tried to rest easy while we drove, but the jouncing of the cab didn't make it possible.

The Flood Warehouse had a gigantic neon sign on the top of it but most of it was obscured in the cloud layer that hovered above the city. It cast a bluish pall over the square structure below it, extending to the ramshackle tenement buildings that flanked it on either side.

I got out on the corner, the pain from my side drawing my face tight. The cabbie looked at me curiously. "You want I should wait?"

This time I handed him a twenty. "Give me an hour. Can you sit it out?"

"So I park with the doors locked, the lights off and the meter running. For this kind of dough, why not?"

"Yeah, why not?" I slid out of the cab.

"Hey, mister?"

"What?"

"You in trouble?"

"Not me, buddy. Somebody else, but not me."

"Like I could call the cops or something?"

"Like in an hour you do that if I'm not back."

"Hey, mister."

"What?"

He saw my face in the lights then. "Nothing. I'll wait for you."

James Harvey had an import house dealing in Chinese specialties right next to the warehouse. It was an old three-story building renovated years ago to accommodate a business and nothing had changed since. Although the area was littered with refuse from the other places, his was a neat establishment with a garage on one side and a wholesale grocery on the other. The few cartons of trash were neatly stacked awaiting pickup and the only smell from the place was a pleasant one that reminded me of an old country store with open herb containers when I was a kid.

Beside the wholesale grocery place were two buildings with boarded-up windows and notices of condemnation tacked to their doors. I walked past them, but knew damn well Malcolm Turos wouldn't take a chance in a place kids could use for nesting pads in a love bout or bums could stake a claim to.

So I went on past the Flood Warehouse trying to think like Turos would, getting further away from the cab that was only a dark blob on the end of the block now.

I smelled Tom Lee Foy's business long before I was near it. It was a smell that brought back all the times I had chiseled the prunelike nuts out of Charlie Hop Soong on Columbus Avenue and for fun we called him *Leechee Chuck,* a fat old

Chinaman with a penchant for kids who let us swipe handfuls when he would have given them to us anyway.

Either Tom Lee Foy did a hell of a business in litchi nuts or he processed them there himself, because they laid an aroma over the section even the driving rain couldn't wash away. I hugged the side of the buildings where the shadows were and took my time about locating the possible spots he could be in.

The river wasn't far off and any prevailing wind would be from there. On one side of Foy's place was an electrical winding business that would cut off any gust of air, but on the other there were four tenements still standing and there were no posted notices on their doors. One even had a sign outside that read "ROOMS TO LET." Two others I wasn't interested in. One had a baby carriage standing on the porch and the other had a cat sitting lazily on the railing with a kid's bicycle behind it.

The one in the middle was a little too innocuous, even with the night light burning behind the glass front door. It was a place where only one person would be, with no prying eyes on other floors to observe him.

The rain and the thunder covered any noise I made as I went around the place, going over the fence to get into the yard in back of the house. I found the two trip wires and knew I had found Malcolm Turos too. He wasn't taking any chances, but didn't have the ideal setup to rig a carefully concealed alarm. He did what I would have done too and I was looking for it.

Upstairs someplace he was sitting, not realizing that everything had blown on him, believing all avenues covered . . . Vey Locca dead, Teish under guard by a stupid compatriot who was ingratiating himself with a foreign power by playing the patsy. He was well hidden and surrounded by traps that could alert him to any intruder and when he was ready he could move at his own leisure.

Outside the world could fall apart and he'd be there to pick up the pieces.

He thought.

I grinned into the night and the rain and felt my way around the windows until I came to the one I wanted with a fine thread of wire not quite in place.

I cut it, pretty certain that any electrical warning device he had installed wasn't more than a hasty job to keep out the locals than anyone looking for him. I got the window up, climbed over the sill and dropped inside soundlessly.

From outside I got the same smell Turos had and closed the window in back of me. There was something else too, something not bred in a Chinese import house. I sniffed the air, located it and remembered what it was. Sarim Shey had smoked a cigar like that when I saw him in the alley of the hotel.

I took the .45 out and held it in my hand, then put it under my coat a second to muffle the click as I thumbed the hammer back. Little by little my eyes were getting used to the blackness and when I could pick out the vague shapes of the furniture in the room I started to make my way across it.

And I found Sarim Shey.

He wasn't much now. He was a dead body still clutching his chest, knees drawn up in agony, lying in a fetal position on the floor, his skin just beginning to cool. A chair was overturned beside him and when I felt his neck I found the nylon cord around it that was buried beneath the flesh and knew he died the hard way and I didn't have any feeling for him at all. He had come to demand and died instead. He was in the way of the grand program and just another one considered expendable and it could all be blamed on the viciousness that lay at the heart of the city.

I heard the feet on the stairs and straightened up so fast my side felt as if someone had a knife in it. I had to hold still until the rush of pain subsided, step across to the door that opened off the front room and wait there. A thin line of light seeped across the opening on the bottom of the sill and I put my hand on the knob, waiting.

He didn't expect me. He was almost at the bottom, the man in the gray suit who could disappear in a crowd at any time, an average guy with glasses and a briefcase and eyes so bright they looked like an animal's.

I should have shot first instead of enjoying the moment. I should have let one go before the pain got me in the side and doubled me up like Sarim was on the floor behind me.

Malcolm Turos had his one second to do what he had to do and the little gun with the silencer appeared in his hand like magic and made a soft plopping sound and I felt the bullets tug at my clothes and one tear across the top of my shoulder.

The same pain that doubled me saved me because he thought I'd throw myself to one side instead of going under the barrage and aimed for there. The look on his face was one of pure joy and the scar at the base of his throat puckered as he let out a hoarse yell of triumph as he recognized me and thought my gift of a bullet in the neck to him was being returned in full.

But he missed and instinct squeezed the trigger of the .45 in my fist and sheer professionalism and hours of practice put the single slug where I wanted it to go and the silenced rod flew out of his hand into the room and as he went for it I brought the butt of the .45 down on the top of his head with a sickening thud and he fell stretched out on the floor.

There was Rondine and there was Lily Tornay. There were others who would hear and think many times before they attempted the same thing again. In Moscow the dossier with my name would have another page added to it and the one who had me assigned as a project would find excuses to beg off and whoever else took it would know who had gone before them and how. They would never be able to operate with the efficiency that was expected of them, and in their turn they would die too.

I found the roll of nylon cord in his pocket and took my time about tying him up. I added a few touches of my own that would insure the muscular reaction of a spasm in a time not too long from now. I tied his hands and feet behind him and as Malcolm Turos regained consciousness I was putting the final loop around his neck that would choke him to death long before he was found and nobody would care at all.

He was expendable too.

There would be complaints and I would have to answer questions, but they would get more infrequent and less insistent as the stories were told.

That's what happens when you play the odds. Somebody wins, somebody loses.

First I'd see a doctor, then I would go to Rondine. She would want to know about it too. Not right away. It would take a few days before I let anyone know.

Malcolm Turos was looking up at me with horrified eyes as the rope bit into his neck. "Kismet, buddy," I said and left him there.

I went back into the rain and walked the long street down to the cab. I woke the driver up and climbed into the back. My side was giving me hell.

"Let's go," I said.

More Mystery from SIGNET

☐ **THE MEPHISTO WALTZ by Fred Mustard Stewart.** A masterpiece in suspense and quiet (the most deadly) horror. Only the strongest will resist its subtly diabolic power. (#Q4184—95¢)

☐ **THE MAN WHO LOVED WOMEN by Ernest Bornemann.** A contentedly married man suddenly finds his marriage disrupted and himself involved in a menage à trois affair. (#Q4223—95¢)

☐ **THE SECRET SOLDIER by John Quigley.** A unique mystery set in Formosa that deals with underworld and smuggling dope. (#T4131—75¢)

☐ **THE CHAIRMAN by Jay Richard Kennedy.** A teacher turned agent is sent on a dangerous assignment to China to find a "destruction machine." A major motion picture starring Gregory Peck. (#Q4007—95¢)

☐ **DOUBLE AGENT by John Huminik.** The true and extraordinary story of a young American scientist's double life as a Russian spy and a counter spy for the F.B.I. (#T3693—75¢)

THE NEW AMERICAN LIBRARY, INC., P.O. Box 2310, Grand Central Station, New York, New York 10017

Please send me the SIGNET BOOKS I have checked above. I am enclosing $_____(check or money order—no currency or C.O.D.'s). Please include the list price plus 15¢ a copy to cover mailing costs. (New York City residents add 6% Sales Tax. Other New York State residents add 3% plus any local sales or use taxes.)

Name_____

Address_____

City_____State_____Zip Code_____

Allow at least 3 weeks for delivery